Isaac Unbound

Isaac Unbound

A Life of Reconciliation

PAUL J. CITRIN

RESOURCE *Publications* · Eugene, Oregon

ISAAC UNBOUND
A Life of Reconciliation

Copyright © 2023 Paul J. Citrin. All rights reserved. Except for brief quotations in critical publications or reviews, no part of this book may be reproduced in any manner without prior written permission from the publisher. Write: Permissions, Wipf and Stock Publishers, 199 W. 8th Ave., Suite 3, Eugene, OR 97401.

Resource Publications
An Imprint of Wipf and Stock Publishers
199 W. 8th Ave., Suite 3
Eugene, OR 97401

www.wipfandstock.com

PAPERBACK ISBN: 978-1-6667-7747-5
HARDCOVER ISBN: 978-1-6667-7748-2
EBOOK ISBN: 978-1-6667-7749-9

07/07/23

In Honor of
Susan M. Citrin
For Her Boundless Love and Support

Contents

Acknowledgments		ix
A Note to the Reader		xi
Prologue		1
I	Shattering the Jug of Blessing	3
II	Weaning and Dreaming	10
III	Seeking Ishmael	21
IV	Ishmael's Narrative	27
V	Moriah: Recurring Nightmare	38
VI	Twin Tales	46
VII	The School of Sham V'Avar	52
VIII	Reconciliation	58
IX	Meditation and Meeting	62
X	Comfort	68
XI	Returning	75
XII	Contraction	81
XIII	Covenant Bearers	93
XIV	The Interment of Abraham	96
XV	Birth and Brit Milah	98
XVI	Wrestlings	103
XVII	Differences and Distances	110
XVIII	Searching	115
XIX	Guile and Guilt	119
XX	Opening the Eyes of the Blind	124

Contents

XXI	A Stew of Blessing	130
XXII	Deceit for Destiny	134
XXIII	Wholeness Unbound	140

About the Author   143

Acknowledgments

My thanks go to the honest and trusted people who read drafts of *Isaac Unbound* and made many constructive suggestions: Rabbi Connie Golden, Bruce Grossman, Glorya Hale, Richard Hammer, and Susan Keith. I owe special gratitude to my son, Aaron Citrin, for his discerning eye, his astute ear for language, and his editorial suggestions, which have enhanced this book.

A Note to the Reader

TORAH IS TERSE. WE may even call its narrative laconic. Torah frequently presents few details of personality and motive. Brevity and absence of specifics lead the reader of Torah to ask questions both about what is reported and about glaring lacunae. This book is the author's attempt to fill in the blanks on the life of Isaac. In order to grasp the questions, insights, imaginings, and understanding of the author, he makes the respectful request of the reader to read (or reread) Genesis 17:1—28:9.

The language in this text is not "biblical" in the sense of sounding like King James English or like the Jewish Publication Society's 1917 version. The author uses contemporary English idiom without slang in order to make the novel accessible for the reader. Descriptions of the landscape, customs, and character traits are intended to carry the biblical flavor of *Isaac Unbound*.

Prologue

THESE ARE THE STORIES of Isaac, the son of Abraham and Sarah. Various people in Isaac's life partake in these stories, but the tablet of their telling is often in Isaac's head. We know from ancient sacred Scriptures that Isaac would go out into the field at twilight *la-su'ach*. *La-su'ach* is a strange and elastic word. *Sia'ch* means shrubbery and bushes. It may be the case that Isaac found in the northern Negev the spirit of plants to be soothing and renewing. In the cooling desert twilight, shrubs exhale the singular, sharp fragrance of oneness and existence. Their collective breath may refresh one who carries the shards and broken pieces of emotional internal life.

La-su'ach means to meditate. When the sun descends into the Great Sea at twilight, it is neither day nor night. It is the time in between. Could we not say that *la-su'ach*, to meditate, is the twilight of consciousness? It is not only the clearing of the mind but also the entrance to an inner space of being. One ventures that the liminal place of *la-su'ach* may bring a person to a realm of calm and perhaps to the wholeness called *shalom*. Yet, like the setting sun at twilight sinking into the unsettled sea, the path of meditation may still sink into the roiling turmoil of a pained spirit.

This reality brings us to the third meaning of *la-su'ach*, to converse. *Sichah* is conversation. *La-su'ach* means to express what is in the bag of human life experience and to listen to how your interlocutors understand your story and how they fit into it. These facets of *la-su'ach* may bring healing and repair. Conversing is a period of twilight, of betweenness. It is a pendulum of relationship as we speak and listen, ask and evaluate, opine and relinquish judgment. If one is diligent and courageous enough to be in honest conversation, and if one opens the door to sources of wisdom beyond oneself, revelations yield insight and direction for a life of wholeness.

Isaac has had moments in his life that have made him feel shattered and broken. He has had long periods when he has felt torn and rent to pieces instead of feeling confident and tightly woven. His pursuit of *la-su'ach*, walking at dusk among shrubbery, turning inward, and conversing with those close to him, is entirely about this quest for personal repair and wholeness.

Some of Isaac's brokenness is rooted in the soil of family conflict that preceded his birth. He is, nevertheless, urgent to repair disconnections. The shadow that both darkens and defines Isaac's outlook is Abraham's intention to offer him as a sacrifice to God. His early relationship with his father and his father's God is radically altered. Isaac also has to interact with the locals of Canaan. Jealousy, fear, and miscommunication undermine the potential for intertribal harmony. Isaac seeks to bridge the chasm of hatred. The most difficult challenge for Isaac, and indeed for each one of us, is to align the values he proclaims with his choices and actions. Isaac, nearing his life's end, attains this alignment by admitting his blindness to realities within himself, in his family, and beyond.

Isaac's story is comprised of many recollections, reflections, encouragements, and confessions. These stories describe his struggle for life and growth. Isaac, like each of us, is unique, but we are much like Isaac as we seek to mend that which is shattered in our lives, in our families, and beyond. And so, you are invited to read stories by and about Isaac that are based on Scripture, *midrash* (rabbinic interpretations), and modern imagination. Come, hear the voices of Abraham and Sarah, Eliezer and Ishmael, Rebekah and Esau, and Isaac himself. As we read these stories, the twilight rays of repair, renewal, and hope may shine upon our lives.

I

Shattering the Jug of Blessing

ELIEZER, AS SARAH'S ONLY son, I will never forget that you performed the sacred ritual no one in the family was ready to do. We were engulfed by blackness when we shut into the grave the remains of Sarah, whose face had shone upon us for decades. Once we sealed Sarah's tomb in the cave of Machpelah, each of us stood paralyzed. Any glimpse of the future without Sarah eluded us.

It was denial that prevented Abraham or me from performing the shattering of her water jug. Sarah's sudden death and our mountainous grief kept us from affirming our loss with the required act. But you, loyal Eliezer, knew our anguish. You shared it as an adopted family member. You did what was necessary, moving with the strength of love beyond mere duty.

You took upon yourself the ritual, which, far beyond the weight of the jug, was encumbered with the family's searing pain. When you hoisted the jug over your head and spoke the words, "Shaddai, Your judgments are just and true," you offered up our hearts as well. You smashed the jug inside the entrance to the cave. Shards flying and crashing penetrated the walls of our numbness. You shattered our denial. We could begin to mourn for Sarah and for ourselves.

As the shards lay at the mouth of the tomb, Father peered into an undefined distance. He wore an entranced look we have at times noted over the years. He spoke so softly. We were like eavesdroppers, yet his words were a record and reminder for us.

Abraham murmured, "Milcah, my brother Nahor's wife, made the water jug as a wedding gift for Sarai. Sarai, as she was called in her youth, was a priestess of the moon god of Ur. Milcah was a priestess as well, but she was senior to Sarah and had already been married for several years. Such was the custom in Ur for a married priestess to fashion a water jug as a gift for a newly betrothed priestess. The wide mouth of the jug allowed beams of the full moon to penetrate and sanctify the water.

"Two days before we left Ur, Sarah and I had the only screaming fight of our marriage. She insisted on taking the jug with her. I told her that since she was no longer a priestess of an impossible no-god whose being waxes and wanes, she would not need the jug with its painted moon symbols. But she insisted she could neither leave Ur nor serve El Shaddai, our one true God, unless the jug remained with her. Taking the jug was a compromise, a trade of loyalty and belief for keeping the priestess' container of healing and blessing. And now, the jug is shattered, and Sarah is gone. Eliezer, I ask you, where is the healing, and who will sprinkle us with hope and blessing?"

I have no doubt, Father, that your question to Eliezer was laden with the weight of your and Sarah's past. Wherever you set up your tents, in Shechem at Alon Moreh, near Beth El, or at Be'er Sheva, mother sprinkled water from the jug over the ground. Peace and blessings would then abide in our tents, not that the harmony was ever unbroken. Jealousy, disappointment, and even danger did fragment our lives. Yet, as long as Mother was able to dip into the jug and sprinkle sacred water about the tents and over the ground, healing and wholeness grew again out of the alkaline soil of our trials.

Abraham's gaze into the past and his musings continued as we stood at the mouth of Machpelah.

"The one and only time that jug did not stand at the entrance to Sarah's living quarters was when we went down to Egypt to escape famine in Canaan. It was several days into our journey, as we reached Sinai's coastal road, that I noticed the absence of the water jug. Neither the pack animals nor our wagons bore it. When I asked Sarah where it was, she said she buried it among the roots of the oak of Mamre. She said she was sure El Shaddai would protect us in Egypt and would again return us to Canaan. Only El Shaddai could guard us in Egypt, that land of debauchery and death-worship. Despite her reliance on El Shaddai, I felt compelled to tell the Egyptians she was my sister rather than my wife. Pharaoh would have me killed in order to take my alluring wife. If he thought Sarah was my sister, he would take her and leave me be. I took a less than courageous stance. Even a man who claims to trust in God can suffer corrosive doubt. Sarah acquiesced because she knew me and because her confidence in El Shaddai was greater than mine. Indeed, she was correct. El Shaddai shriveled Pharaoh's manhood every time he tried to approach Sarah. She laughed as she described Pharaoh's member as a 'wrinkled new-born mouse and just as timid.' His frustrated ardor for Sarah was soon surpassed by his desire for us to leave the country. He loaded us with gold, grain, and rich raiment and had his people hurry us to the Sinai boundary. When we returned to Alon Moreh, Sarah dug up the jug, filled it with water from the well, and set it by her tent door to allow the evening's moonbeams to stream into the water. The morning found Sarah sprinkling water from the jug throughout our camps. We felt the wholeness of returning home descend on us like dew."

My father's admission of his doubt about El Shaddai astounded me. Did he question the faithfulness of the promises of the Most High? Was Abraham so tepid in his convictions? Did he feel more vulnerable than I had imagined? As he stood next to me at Mother's tomb—I in middle age and he in his dotage—I grasped that his journey had been one of struggle and doubt. Since Moriah, and with all the demands he placed on me to uphold the Covenant of El Shaddai, I never dreamed his faith would waver throughout his life. Now, in the depths of his grief for Mother, he turns to you, Eliezer, and asks, "Where is healing?"

Isaac Unbound

He has relied on you, Eliezer, as the senior servant and the managing partner of his household. It occurs to me now that you were, for him, the physical embodiment of El Shaddai's support. As is your name, "My God is help," so have you helped Abraham, thereby assisting the divine purposes. Sarah brought wholeness to Father's life, and you were always present to gather the pieces of what was unavoidably broken. At the tomb of Sarah, you did the shattering. Abraham looks to you to bring wholeness out of what is fragmented.

Your solution for Father was truly brilliant. You said to him, "There is no wholeness in being alone, nor solace in solitude. Ask Keturah, Sarah's chief maid, to be your wife. She is worthy. Sarah would approve and encourage you."

A year passed until Abraham listened to and acted on your advice, Eliezer. He seems sturdier now and more sure of himself. Keturah is a balm to him, a reviving incense. He has come back to himself. Today I heard him say he feels blessed, that he has got it all. Could we not say, Eliezer, that this is healing in the fullest sense?

This morning, Eliezer, before your departure for Paddan Aram, Father's sense of being blessed led him to consider my well-being and my future. You surprised me when you told me, Eliezer, that Father had charged you with the mission to find me a wife in Paddan Aram. Your news stoked the flame of burning questions that time had reduced to embers in my heart. Why had Father never spoken to me about marriage during the past two decades of my life? He never approached local chieftains to negotiate a betrothal with one of their daughters. How could Abraham expect El Shaddai to fulfill the promise to make him a great nation without finding a wife for me? As I near my fortieth year, am I not able to seek a wife without intervention? I could have gone to Paddan Aram myself, seeing that Canaanite women were not satisfactory to Father and Mother. And where was Mother's voice?

At times, I have felt that Father doubted me to the point where I wondered if I was up to bearing the Covenant. The future is beclouded, and my vision of it is blurred. Mother's death has wrapped a benumbing sheath around my heart. Too many times in the past, I have felt cowed, unable to act. Now, the debris of passivity clogs my blood and eddies in pools of despair.

Perhaps El Shaddai is testing my reliance on divine compassion. If you, Eliezer, are Abraham's surrogate, then you are El Shaddai's servant as well. I trust you not only for your proven wisdom and concern but also because of your acute perception of El Shaddai's voice. Eliezer, you are my hope and comfort, as you have been since my earliest days. I know, with El Shaddai's guidance, you will set me on the path I will walk. Though you are quite elderly to be imposed upon with a trek through mountains and desert, I know you will find a fitting wife for me.

As I watch you moving eastward, leading ten of Father's camels laden with gifts, stepping with a rhythmic gait, I see you as part of the landscape. You are returning now to the land from which you came, the region of Damascus. That is where Father first met you on his way from Haran.

The story I have heard is that while Abraham was teaching about El Shaddai at a village well not far from Damascus, he saw you at the edge of the group that had gathered. You were gazing at him intently. You seemed to drink in his words. Abraham would say later that he felt you emerging from the desert of your pagan self, covered with the dust of superstition and parched for the water of truth. Father told me how you approached him with one simple question: "Beside belief, what does your El Shaddai ask of us humans?" When you heard Father's answer, "Only to walk in righteousness," you prostrated yourself at his feet. Abraham said it was as though you had placed your soul in his charge. You joined him and Mother for a new life in a land to the west. Father made you "zekan beito," the senior servant, retainer, and manager of his worldly goods and affairs. You became his other self, even as he relied on you to do what was right and necessary.

Eliezer, you became part of our household and of Canaan by choice and commitment. I do not fear that your return to your homeland will, for a moment, prevent you from your task or from your return. On the other hand, I was born in this land. In all but religion, I am a Canaanite. I am of this place. I learned of El

Shaddai in the tents of Abraham and Sarah. Despite my status as a homeborn, one of Sarah's very flesh and blood, I am far from certain I am able to be as faithful as you have been.

The difference between Abraham and you, on the one hand, and me, on the other, is that your discovery of El Shaddai intoxicated you both with faithful zeal. I dutifully learned what Father and you taught me, but I have been touched neither by my personal awareness of El Shaddai's presence nor by the intimacy of receiving a divine word. So, I doubt. It is not a doubt in El Shaddai's reality or even the Covenant.

My question to myself is whether I have the emotional, moral, and spiritual capacity to bear my part of the Covenant. At times, I have thought of leaving this land for Aram Naharaim, where two rivers water the fertile valley and where constantly digging wells is an unknown effort. Since the horror of Moriah, I have longed for a new Covenant with El Shaddai, in which we agree to cease demands, to commit to mutual disengagement. I could shun El Shaddai if El Shaddai would ignore me.

This, of course, will not come to pass. Father and you will see to that in some way I have yet to imagine. One thing is clear to me. I will pursue the Covenant with El Shaddai in my own way. I will define for myself what it means to "walk in righteousness."

I do not need any grand gestures or audacious actions on my part. Does El Shaddai want me to pursue kings in battle to demonstrate His power? I do not think that is His assignment for me. Am I required by El Shaddai to save cities, to plead and bargain like a camel merchant in Be'er Sheva? I already know El Shaddai's justice is beyond my understanding. The only charge I will accept is the broad, hope-filled call, "Be a blessing!"

I cannot myself be a blessing to nations, cities, or clans. That may come in time as our tribe grows. For me, blessing comes person by person, through struggle with individual selves—with my own being and with other beings. There are so many severed relationships. Our lives are strewn with shattered hopes. Fear is a forceful hammer. Shards and fragments lie about waiting for repair. Like my mother, Sarah, I believe repair—mending and healing—is my task. If El Shaddai is listening, and even if He is not, this I declare to be my part of the Covenant: mending and healing. May the God of Abraham guide me and be my strength, thereby also becoming the God of Isaac.

Yesterday, when I stood in this spot, the ground was cracked after the sun had dried the night's rain puddles. Now this earth is a mosaic of varying sizes and shapes of damp mud. If it rains again today, those cracks—those mud shards—will disappear into an amorphous puddle that will return the mud to a kind of oneness. At this moment, sprouting up between the cracks are wisps of new grass—vital, tender green shoots. There is something about the frail boldness of their appearance that reminds me of Mother's laughter, which is spontaneous and encouraging. I will take this as a sign from Sarah and El Shaddai to be a blessing in my own way. If I can move beyond the burdens of the broken past, gathering shards, giving blessing, I too will laugh again as Mother did.

II

Weaning and Dreaming

A RECURRING DREAM WEAVES itself through my nights. I am standing by an olive tree at the edge of the field. A few stars are out in the tar-thick darkness. Crickets chirp, and a roving jackal now and then lets out a prideful howl. The breeze is a diligent messenger, carrying from the tents the music of flute, drum, and laughter. I barely know what sound to follow. There are so many that I am dazed until I look eastward.

Over the hills of Moab, the moon rises. It ascends rapidly above the valley of the Jordan. This night is the middle of the month of Aviv, when the full moon of spring rules heaven and earth. There is neither modesty nor reticence in the moon of Aviv, whose presence is royal. She gathers the sounds of the night under her rule so that braying donkeys, human shouts, and baying jackals become a wordless song of hope and fullness. Her brilliance reminds me of the polished bronze mirrors Egyptian traders sell. Yet, it is not vanity that this full moon beams forth. Her warm, penetrating light reveals compassion.

As the Aviv moon reaches her zenith, the fields seem as distinct as they are by day. The weighty barley is ripe. Heavy stalks bow with a promise of fullness for humans and beasts. There will be no scarcity, no reason for envy or greed. Each will have his portion, every need answered, with an abundant remainder of grain for parching or later planting. I stand gazing at the illuminated field, taking in the living night. A figure appears. His back is to me. I see his curly black hair, which tumbles down the back of his head and fans out, covering his neck. Over his shoulder, he carries a quiver of arrows. He reaches, takes out an arrow, and brings it to his bow. Now, he fits the arrow to the bow string. He tilts his right shoulder back, pointing toward the earth. His left hand is at the bow, and his outstretched arm directs the arrowhead at the moon. He pulls back the bow string and arrow, then releases the taut power.

The arrow flies upward. It hits the edge of the Aviv moon, knocking off a golden sliver from the disk. He pulls another arrow from the quiver with a sure, swift draw. He fits the arrow and again sends it skyward. Another thin piece of moon is struck off by the arrow. He shoots three more arrows at the moon, who, each time, yields a shard of herself. Her light is not diminished, but her edge has become serrated with intermittent dark spots.

Just as the young man reaches for a sixth arrow, a voice yells out of the darkness, "Wild ass, be gone!" Immediately, the young archer turns into an onager and gallops southward to the wilderness.

This is my recurring dream. I used to beg you, Eliezer, to tell me its meaning. Each time you would say to me, "Interpretations are the property of the dreamer alone." On this refusal, Eliezer, you always stood firm. Yet, I had a sense you knew the true meaning of the dream but wanted me to decode it for myself. There is one certainty I have always carried like a sack on my back: the certainty that the dream was unfinished and was bidding me to respond in some way. That is why I have never ceased pressing you to interpret the dream every time it would fill my head.

You never relented in your silence, Eliezer, except once, years ago. You said to me in a quiet, firm voice, "I think you should ask Abraham to tell you about the feast he made for your weaning." What an odd comment, I thought at the time. Why should I care about an event beyond my memory? Despite my being there, I was blank like an empty clay tablet. But the dream would not abandon me, and you refused to discuss it. Finally, I did as you suggested. I went to Abraham and asked him to tell me about my weaning feast.

Abraham did not refuse me, but when he heard my request, a look of pain came over him. I could not guess how deep was the cistern of his sadness. He said, "I am sure it was Eliezer who sent you to me. He knows my pain and would not subject me to draw it up unless he judged you need to know. I trust him more than I trust myself because he has always been a pursuer of love and kindness. Come into the tent, and I will tell you.

"First, you should know," my father began, "that you were not so easy to wean. At eighteen months, your mother tried to have you drink from a cup, as most children like to do, but you pushed it away. Then, you amazed me by uttering your first word. When you pushed the cup away, you yelled, 'Shaddai!' I smiled to myself that in your frustration, you called out to our God as your inaugural word. Then my smile turned to laughter when I realized that 'Shaddai' also means 'my breasts!' You were not calling upon God as His youngest believer. You were demanding what you thought was rightfully yours: Sarah's breasts. You and your mother shared such a bond that was never truly loosened, even after you were weaned.

"It took your mother a fair amount of effort to wean you. That is partly because I was pushing her to move you from infancy to childhood. She succeeded for both of you by giving you extra time in her tent and by holding you close to her each time you finished drinking a cup of goat milk. Two months before your second birth anniversary, you were weaned. I never heard you say 'Shaddai' again until you were a lad of four, when you asked me if El Shaddai also moved here from Haran. Once it was clear your weaning was complete, your mother and I planned a feast to honor the occasion.

"We set the date for the feast on the full moon of Aviv, the second anniversary of your birth. When I brought you into the Covenant, circumcising you on your eighth day, I kept that as a day of private contentment. Sarah and I wanted no public feasting. For your weaning, we could no longer resist giving full expression to our happiness and amazement that you arrived so late in our lives.

We decided to make a huge feast of many courses for numerous guests.

"When word of your birth became known in Canaan, a rumor began to ripple around the land like sand on a wind-blown dune. People would tell each other, with the knowing look of those who are bored with their own ignorance, that your real father must be Abimelech, the king of Gerar.

"It was well known that when your mother and I sojourned in his country, he took her into his abode intending to make her a concubine. That happened about seven months before your birth. What the Canaanites did not know—for certainly Abimelech would not share the story—is that El Shaddai did to him what He had done to Pharaoh when we were in Egypt. El Shaddai took all appetite away from the Philistines—from the king, his courtiers, and even from their women. Had Abimelech not released your mother, his fate and that of his kingdom would have been sterility of loin and the vanishing of urge. Death would have been the judgment upon Gerar. Abimelech never touched Sarah.

"He sent us away with reparation gifts and even invited us to settle wherever we wished in his land. I felt his anger and hatred despite his visible effort to make things right between us. We moved on toward Be'er Sheva, which was still under the control of Abimelech. We dug wells and prospered.

"Sarah and I wanted to dispel the idea that Abimelech sired you. Your eyes are my eyes, and your chin is just like mine. One look at you would be enough for anybody to see whose son you are. Your mother and I also thought that a feast made enmity disperse as the morning sun evaporated dawn's mist. So we invited Abimelech and his general, Phicol, and all of his courtiers and their families. We asked Melchizedek of Shalem, High Priest of El Elyon, to honor us with his presence. Ephron, Aner, and Eshkol, with their wives and children, accepted our call and came to us from Kiryat Arba. You can imagine that with all of their families and servants, as well as Hagar, your brother Ishmael, Eliezer, and our three hundred retainers, your mother and I were hosting a great feast that brought a thousand guests.

"Our guests slowly arrived in their finest garments, as varied as the expressions on their faces. Abimelech wore a robe dyed with the deep purple of the sea hare. His face bore a sneer, almost a grimace, as though some putrid odor assaulted his nostrils. Melchizedek, in contrast to Abimelech, wore a look of pure delight, which made his natural goat-hair tunic seem to shine. Ephron, the Hittite, in his patterned and checkered coat, looked smug with himself as if he possessed favors to dispense as whim would engender.

"All of our distinguished guests came with curiosity about parents of such advanced age. They expected to see wrinkled, liver-spotted skin and bent backs. What they found was renewed energy, clear skin, and strength in the back and arms. You, my son, with the help of El Shaddai, also known as Harachaman, the Merciful Master of the Uterus, gave us back our youth. Indeed, our vigor surprised them more than that we had you at the withering season of our lives. When they saw how our wrinkles had become smooth skin again, their haughty, condescending looks turned to amiable expressions.

"As the sun set, the feast began. The women and their children sat in front of Sarah's tent. Around the tamarisk I had planted sat the men on their sleeping rolls. Our camp became, as it were, an expansive inn. Servants brought out olives basking in oil and spices, along with warm bread. The heat imparted by the fire as well as by the bread and wine molded the air of formality and judgment into one of radiant relaxation. People began to joke and laugh. They urged each other to take more. Curds, butter, and fresh bread were added to the feast, with wine skins replenished and circulated. Flutes were brought to smiling lips, and drums were embraced. There would be a few hours of music and wine while fifty lambs finished their time in the coals.

"The assembly was becoming ever more comfortable and lighthearted when Eliezer took me aside. His frown betrayed worry. I excused myself to see what was bothering him. He said, 'Abraham, my master, I have never known you to eat or to provide food for others without blessing El Shaddai's gracious gifts. Tonight, you did not bless. Also, I would have expected this feast of Isaac's weaning to be an occasion to offer sacrifice. Tonight, you did not sacrifice. I do not understand, and I worry whether El Shaddai will understand this opulent display, which lacks nothing but your testimony and gratitude to Him.'

"Eliezer may call me 'Master' with a tone of reverence and love, but he has never hesitated to speak his mind to me. Of course, he was correct to wonder about the absence of my usual devotion to El Shaddai. I explained to him that my purpose was to bring these contentious inhabitants of Canaan together in fellowship. I did not want to give any of the leaders, each of whom clings to his own gods as a matter of tribal pride, a reason to think they were invited for an ulterior motive. My effort to bear witness to El Shaddai's goodness is to show that the true way of God is openness. It is in sharing the fruits of this land together, especially in the midst of our personal joys and sorrows. As long as the presence of Philistines and Canaanites in the land has not exhausted Shaddai's patience, I must seek accommodation on a human level. This I do particularly for Isaac's sake, for he will dwell among them for a long time. Eliezer praised my efforts toward reconciliation, and we returned to our guests.

"Soon, the roasted lambs would be pulled from their snug beds of glowing coals. You could sense the urgency of appetite that no amount of olives, curd, or bread could curb. Before the lambs were brought forth in all their beckoning fat, it was time to present you to the company, my son.

"From out of the tent of women, your mother brought you to me in front of the fire before hundreds of men. All voices and sounds ceased. Sarah had strengthened her determination to release you from the intimacy and indulgences of her tent. With a firm voice, she announced, 'I present my son, Isaac, my firstborn and my only son, whom I love well, to his father and to the tribe he is destined to lead.' I stood behind you, my hands on your shoulders, as you faced the assembly of men of diverse gods and practices. As is the way of Canaan, a cheer broke out simultaneously around the fire: 'Yechi Yitzchak, yechi, yechi, yechi!' Thus you were wished a long life by all our guests.

"I had just returned to my place by the fire, and you were still standing at your place when your brother Ishmael rushed forward. You always adored him and thrived on every flutter of attention he sent your way. When he came up behind you and lifted your robe, you began to giggle and laugh. He exposed your private parts and the mark of the Covenant.

"'This is the claim of Sarah's firstborn to the Covenant,' proclaimed Ishmael, as he flicked your member up repeatedly with the back of two fingers. You laughed while I was too stunned to speak. Ishmael declared, 'I was thirteen when I was brought into the Covenant. Now that takes commitment! But this little maggot was only eight days old when it was trimmed, and my brother entered the Covenant. He hardly felt it, and this gives him the right to lead our clan!' Just then, the trays of lamb were brought in. The laughter stirred by Ishmael's antics had barely faded. All attention turned from Ishmael to the dripping pink flesh of spring lambs. I was as dumb as a stone after your brother's show, and I hoped Sarah had not noticed. My hope was not justified; Sarah had witnessed Ishmael's crude show. Her face was as dark as a beet. Her eyes flashed a lightening anger contained only by a determined silence. I knew the thunder would burst forth later. For the moment, Sarah did not wish to destroy the celebratory mood.

"After our guests had their fill of lamb, Sarah called all the children to come to her tent with their mothers. She was to distribute hundreds of Land of Canaan cakes, one per child. Early that morning, Saran had ground wheat and barley seeds into a fine yet textured flour. She mixed the flour with olive oil and a measure of honey. When the dough was well mixed, your mother added dried figs and raisins. On the top of these round cakes that rose up in the center, she sprinkled small clusters of pomegranate seeds. Then she baked them.

"These round Land of Canaan cakes, so called by your mother because they contained the seven species indigenous to the land, looked like small, budding breasts. The pomegranate suggested nipples in the middle of the upraised top. This is how the story began to be told—that your mother nursed hundreds of children that day, thereby blessing them. Your mother's milk had dried up months before due to your weaning. What Sarah provided were delicious, sweet, breast-shaped cakes, which delighted the children. When she distributed them, she said, 'Just as we share in these cakes the fruits of our mother, Canaan, may we share this land in peace.'

"The music and laughter continued into the night while sparks from the fire exploded upward as though seeking their place among the stars. Wine skins continued to make the rounds, and the company began to be encircled by bonds of sleep. You, my son, were having a grand time and were very much awake so as not to miss the attention of anyone. Then your brother, Ishmael, reappeared next to you. He took you up on his shoulders while you giggled at the glory of it. 'Come, little brother, let's go into the field, and I'll show you my inheritance is greater than yours!' Before I could say anything, Ishmael was running toward the field with you on his shoulders.

"The full moon of Aviv was high in the sky. Ishmael set you on the ground in front of him. He said, 'Watch, little brother, my arrows will show you how far my inheritance goes.'

"Ishmael drew an arrow from his quiver, pulled it back on the bowstring, and released it, arching above your head. It landed far to the east. Then Ishmael faced west and shot a second arrow that flew above your head a good distance. Once again, your brother sent a third arrow over your head, reflecting moonlight as it sailed to the southern edge of the field. Ishmael was about to shoot a fourth arrow. He turned to face north when he saw Sarah running toward him. She had seen the previous shots and thought your brother was making a sport to kill you. Sarah chased your brother with a scythe, yelling, 'Be off, you wild ass! Get away from my Isaac, wild ass!'

"That night, your mother insisted I banish Ishmael and his mother, Hagar, from our tents. No amount of explaining or pleading for my precious Ishmael helped. Sarah was determined. 'That one, that wild ass, will not inherit with my son!' So the next dawn following your weaning feast, I gave Hagar a skin of water so large she had to drag it on a rope over her shoulder. I gave her bread to feed herself and your brother. I told her to head toward Paran, where springs bubble up in the midst of wilderness. I left her far beyond the edge of our camp and thus exiled my firstborn son, Ishmael, your brother.

"It was my greatest sorrow, a burden every bit as painful and strenuous as the water bag Hagar carried. Her water bag made a deep rut in the desert sand and rubble. My pain made a wadi in my soul that no other love, not even you, can fill. That is the story of your weaning feast, my son—a tale I do not choose to repeat or relive."

"Father," I said, "there has always been a wilderness in my life that I never understood until now. My own wasteland is barren even of brambles of sibling struggle and of the oasis that flows out of love between brothers. I have so much, but I have felt this void forever. It has invaded my dreams as well. I am going to seek out Ishmael. I am going to reach out to him to fix a bond I did not break. I need Ishmael in my life."

A long sigh came from Abraham. I was unsure whether it arose from longing or resignation. "My son," Abraham said softly, "I knew this day of your awareness and seeking would come. I will not deter you, but I urge you to gird yourself for disappointment. You have traveled your inner wilderness until now. After you traverse this Negev to the Wilderness of Paran, Ishmael's abode, you may find a greater desolation."

"Father, if the packs I will bear are laden with love, and if my arms are open wide to embrace, I will surely be met with love that overcomes the enmity and jealousy of what is past."

Abraham replied, "Twice I have trekked to Paran to embrace my son Ishmael. Shortly after I endured the shame of exiling my son, I could no longer remain in my tent. Regret and yearning drove me to go to him. The track in the sand that Hagar's waterskin made had not yet been stolen by the winds. I followed that path to Paran until I came to Ishmael's tent. I called to him from my camel. He did not respond, but a woman came out and said, 'Ishmael is not here today. I am Ayesha, his wife.'

"I said to this woman, who was handsome and strong, 'Can you then give me a little bread and water for my return journey?'

"Ishmael's wife said, 'We have neither bread nor water here. Be gone from here.'

"'Tell your husband, Ishmael, that an old man was in the area to call on him. Tell him the old man said his tent ropes are weak.'"

Father told me that he returned to Be'er Sheva more broken-hearted than when he began the journey. It took him two years before he tried again to see my brother.

"I made a second trip to Ishmael. The track was gone, but the way was seared into my mind. I reached Ishmael's tent and called out for him.

"'Ishmael is on a hunting trip. I am his wife, Fatima. What do you want of him?'

"'I merely wish to behold his face. When will he return?' I asked.

"Fatima went into the tent. I heard the low register of a man's voice say, 'I will not again look upon his face while he lives. He set his face against me so that I and my mother nearly died.'

"Fatima came out of the tent with a jug of water and a loaf of bread. She said, 'I do not know when Ishmael will return, but take these provisions. Go home and do not return.'

"Before I turned to go, I asked El Shaddai's blessing on the tents of Ishmael. It seemed to me, as my camel moved northward, that a moaning was following me. Perhaps it was only the wind or an expression from my heart. If you go to seek Ishmael, be ready for an ache that has no balm."

That night, after my father told me the story of my weaning and of his attempts to see Ishmael, my recurring dream visited me. All of the details were the same, except a new element made its appearance. The anonymous voice again yells, "Wild ass, be gone!" The archer flees and turns into an onager. Then, instead of the dream fading, I move from the edge of the field into the standing barley. I am picking up and gathering shards that fell from the rim of the Aviv moon that the archer's arrows chipped off. The shards shine in my hand. They warm me. I think to myself, I will find that onager. When I present to him the shards, he will become the strong archer again. He will embrace me for freeing him from his wildness, for refilling his quiver with shards of compassion and love.

This morning, Eliezer, I awoke with the intention of going to my brother Ishmael. I am resolved to fix what I did not break. I thank you with all my heart for pressing me to speak to Abraham. It has set me on a path of reconciliation. I will return in time to Be'er Sheva to take the wife whom El Shaddai guides you to bring me.

III

Seeking Ishmael

I WONDER, ELIEZER, WHAT you would have said to me if you had been here early this morning when I saddled the camel and loaded a second one with provisions. I know you would have understood with clarity why I went south into the wilderness. Truly, it is my brother I seek. Yet, I am not sure of my deeper purpose for leaving Be'er Sheva. Perhaps the journey itself will lead me to the depths of my heart's yearning.

Before I mounted the camel in the darkness before dawn, I entered Abraham's tent. Sleep had eluded him. He was sitting wrapped in a goat skin. He trembled visibly, and I offered to bring him another robe.

"It is not the morning chill that makes me tremble, my son."

"Father, do not fear for me on the road. El Shaddai will keep His Covenant and watch over me."

"Isaac, I never doubt El Shaddai will do His part, but we must also be cautious and mindful. Please, wake the two servant lads, and take them with you."

"Let them stay here with the asses and help in the sheepfold. I must go alone. I will return to you in peace, Father."

"Isaac, in truth, my trembling is not entirely for your physical safety. That is but a small element of my fear. I am frightened for your spirit, for your devotion to El Shaddai, for your vision of the Covenant."

"What are you saying, Father? Have I not shown myself faithful and worthy of the Covenant as you have taught me?"

"You surely have shown your devotion, and your intention for the future after I am gone seems true."

"Then what is it, Father?"

"Isaac, I fear you will become blind. Love and longing for what cannot be deprives a person of the light of commitment to the future. Do not let the embers of your childhood love for Ishmael burst into a flame that outshines the future. I pray your yearning for a relationship with Ishmael will not cloud your eyes from El Shaddai's Covenant."

"Father, my view of the Covenant is different than yours. My own version of it is no less faithful than yours. My Covenant with Shaddai calls me to seek my brother. I see this clearly, and the vision of my obligation to the future does not dim."

Father's trembling calmed. He beckoned me to kneel in front of him. As I faced him, he placed his hands on my head, and I bowed before him. His voice sounded weary as he blessed me, asking El Shaddai to guard my going and my returning in peace.

I left Father with my mind roving in two directions. My thoughts turn to the east, toward Paddan Aram, as I wonder about Eliezer's progress in finding a wife for me. I pray he is having success, and that she who pleases Eliezer will please me.

As I depart, my thoughts roam southward toward Paran. How can I find Ishmael in a vast wilderness I do not know? If I find my brother, what words will I offer him? How will he receive me? Can shards still be gathered? I know that Eliezer would say to me, "Follow the path; do not falter."

On this late winter's morning, I set out through the grassland, now no longer sparse, that surrounds Be'er Sheva. Winds from the west this year generously shepherd clouds and moisture over Canaan. Abundant rain coaxes the dusty ground to yield nurturing pasture. Ochre earth sprouts fresh green, and low bushes are bejeweled in buds of yellow and pink. Buzzing insects, zigzagging on their missions, echo the energy of a sky so bright it makes me imagine creation's first light. The sun warms me and opens me to the possibilities of claiming that which I lost so long ago. The camels move with seeming determination instead of their usual apathy. The day proclaims hope, nudging me toward confidence. Yet, I am mindful that this is my first journey from home since I returned from the land of Moriah.

The day that Father and I departed for Moriah was also a day of hope and joy. Just to travel far from camp with Father all to myself felt like a pilgrimage. We traveled through the land up to the hill country, the two of us together. We spoke of El Shaddai and how He shows hidden doorways, guides, and demands. Father reminded me of El Shaddai's promise to give all the expanse of Canaan to us and to our family. So thrilling was this time with Father that it was as if I had eaten my fill of honey or bathed in a soothing warm spring.

All was perfect until the third day, when we climbed Moriah. I must push it from my thoughts. I do not want to contemplate it now. Neither can I entirely purge it from my mind.

Shards—that is what fills my mind. I am lying with my head and back on the unyielding stone altar, my body bound in leather thongs. A spreading oak extends its branches over me and the altar. I gaze up into the branches to avoid looking at Father's knife. The boughs reach sideways and send forth branches, which pour themselves into budding twigs. All these stretch out in various directions, crisscrossing and dividing the sky above into shards of blue. A last view of life—these shards of sky fill my vision and my consciousness—until the bleating ram rouses me from the tunnel of my impending end.

Later, Eliezer taught me not to think of what might have been. He pointed my mind to the present and to the future. That is what I must concentrate on as I travel to Ishmael; otherwise shards of doubt and fear will divert me from what I have promised myself to do. The day flees so quickly when one is lost in thought and rocked by the camel's swaying gait. I do not notice exactly when the grass yields to rocks and gravel. Dry stream beds and old canyons were sculpted by water's infrequent but innate persistence. The land looks more gray than ochre. Striations of white salt intrude on the ashen mass of squat table rocks. The shapes are met by lowly scrub plants or an occasional broom tree. In a streambed stands a forlorn acacia.

The sun hurries to the west toward its repose in the Great Sea. Shadows meld into the evening. The heat of the day takes leave without a lingering farewell. The chill of night in the wilderness brings amnesia of the intense light and heat of the day. Stars spill across the sky. Even in their profusion, each seems cold and solitary. I am no different than the stars. The unsaddled camels forage, and I, wrapping myself in a cloak, take a niche in a table rock for a sheltering bed.

When I awake at dawn, a phase keeps going through my head. I repeat to myself, "I have come to claim what I have lost." As I shake off slumber and turn toward the strengthening sun, I realize that this is what I will say to Ishmael when I find him. I have only words for him, not material tributes. I bear no gifts. I only offer myself. I cannot guess if he will hear my plea and help me in my quest. Perhaps he will bar the way to his tent. Nothing is certain. I must continue on this solitary path southward. I imagine you, Eliezer, by my side when my confidence wanes. Your presence in my heart sustains me.

This is the second day of my journey. I continue heading south. Off to the east, the hills of Moab meet the reddish stone of the southern mountains of Edom. There is no sign of Ishmael or of an encampment, though I am aware I have entered the Wilderness of Paran. Here the desert has a different character: it is flat and strewn with gravel. Though the sun is tempered by a winter angle, its glare dominates this wilderness. I wonder if, as Father said, I will find Ishmael's personality overwhelmingly bright and blinding.

Paran is glorious, but it provides little natural shelter. I will not sleep this night under the stars. I will raise my goat skin tent, anchoring its pegs firmly to stand up to the impatient winds rushing to unknown hills and caves. Dates, bread, and water from Be'er Sheva will be my repast. I am so tired that neither the calling jackals nor the moaning wind will steal slumber from me.

Blessedly, my sleep was not disturbed. It was adorned with a dream, which has made me awaken today with calm. The core of my soul is peaceful. I dreamed of a well that was clogged with sand. With my bare hands, I pulled out the earthy debris. A gentle flow of water rose to the mouth of the well, spilling over onto parched ground in all directions. Cracks in the dirt around the well were smoothed and erased by the swelling water. Everything was made one by the water, and there was peace.

Eliezer always said to me that dreaming of a well is an omen for life and peace. What a precious sign it is as I begin my third day of this journey. May Shaddai guide me to Ishmael today, and may finding him result in peace. Without any delay, I shall fold my tent, load and saddle the camels, and continue southward.

The morning is still. I am nodding in the saddle when I hear voices and bleating ahead of me. I look up and see a spot of green. It widens as I get closer. Bushes and scrub trees reside around a source of water, creating an emerald oasis. Shepherds, men and women, are keeping an ample flock from straying into the wilderness beyond the grass. A few tents are planted on one side of the oasis, with smoking fires at their fronts. Shortly, a young shepherd lad looks in my direction. Leaving the girls to look after the sheep, he gathers two boys with him. They run to greet me.

"Welcome, traveler! Come, drink, you and the camels, at our well. Let a little water be taken to wash your feet. We also have bread and meat to revive you. Follow us."

Such enthusiastic hospitality is itself bread and water to my spirit.

"I am honored to follow you and to take refreshment. Blessed is your hospitality."

Soon, we arrive at a shaded, grass-carpeted area next to a pool of water whose bubbling source I could not determine. The lads bring drinking gourds, which they dip into the water of the pool, and they offer me water to drink. The water is cool and sweet, tasting of energy and life. I swallow it. It reminds me of the water from Sarah's jug.

The shepherds remove my sandals and wash the dust from my feet. A bronze tray laden with bread and kid of goat is placed before me. I eat until the memory of three days of trail dates dims. When the shepherd lads judge by my color and my relaxation that I am satiated, a rush of questions pours from them.

"Stranger, what brings you to our Wilderness of Paran? Where do you come from, and what is your destination?"

"I will answer your questions, but first permit me to bless the Master of the bread I have eaten, the one who provides sufficiency for all, El Shaddai. Let me also bless you and this household for your hospitality. Now, if you will first allow me a question, where is your patriarch? Why has he not come forth to greet a wayfarer?"

"Our father has been away with a caravan to Egypt. We expect his return this evening."

"What is your father's name?"

"He is called Ishmael."

"Does he not have a second name? Whose son is he?"

"Our father has no second name. He never speaks of his father. He does joke at times, claiming his true father is a wild ass."

"I look forward to meeting your father. Now, you have filled me so well. Allow me to sleep until Ishmael's return. Then I will reply to his questions and yours."

"To provide a safe bed in a peaceful place is also part of our hospitality. We will wake you when Father arrives."

As I lie down under a tree, my excitement at having found my brother, Ishmael, is temporarily pushed down by my exhaustion. Soon we will meet after so many years. I pray to El Shaddai that our meeting will develop into a love of brothers.

IV

Ishmael's Narrative

A SANDAL POKING THE arch of my bare foot jars my floating sleep. I am brought back to the solid earth of wakefulness by a voice urging me to sit up and drink something. The prodding sandal and voice belong to the same lad who extended hospitality to me last night.

"Please drink this goat milk. There is none sweeter in this wilderness because of the water our goats drink. Then wash yourself and come with me. Father wishes to receive you in his tent."

I take the gourd of milk from the lad, who did not yet know he was providing refreshment to his uncle from Canaan. He is not exaggerating about the milk. It is the purest goat milk I have ever tasted. Tender spring shoots of the animals' diet imparted to the drink a light, dancing flavor. I would have taken more time to savor the renewing milk of the goats of Paran, but the lad nervously alters his gaze from me to the tent door and back to me. I take the last swallow of milk, splash water on my face from a trough outside the tent, and follow the boy.

The camp of Ishmael is seventeen tents around an untiring spring whose pools are carpeted at the edges in grass softer than camel's hair. The chieftain's tent is set back from the others. It is grand, with its speckled goat skins stretched over an area equal to four family tents. What stands out to me in a familiar and perhaps shocking way are the tent's four openings, one facing each direction. That is a most unusual configuration for the tent of a desert chieftain. The only other leader's tent I have seen open to all four directions is Abraham's. Any grains of doubt as to whether I have come to Ishmael's camp are scattered by the winds of recollecting family tradition.

Abraham always modeled for us the value of hospitality to wayfarers. His tent remained open to the four directions for anyone who would seek to enter his shelter for sustenance and repose. Now, I see that this chieftain, Ishmael, surely absorbed our father's example. He had made Abraham's way his way.

I am curious to learn what other of Abraham's teachings Ishmael maintains.

The lad leads me into his father's tent. Ishmael sits on skins, and the thick curly hair I remembered from my dreams still approaches his shoulders. Only now, like his tent skins, his hair and beard are mottled with flecks of gray. Likewise, my heart is streaked with love, fear, and hope. I cannot speak lest I get carried away by the flash flood of my emotions.

"Welcome to Be'er Lachai Ro'i and to my tent," Ishmael offers as he extends his arms toward me with palms facing upward.

I sit as invited, and a servant brings a jug of water and a bowl. He removes my sandals and pours water over my feet.

"Such feet are not the calloused feet of one who traverses the desert with his caravans of merchandise. But this is hardly surprising, because my sons told me you arrived with little else than a few provisions. These are the feet of someone who tends sheep to pass time but who is perhaps the son of a wealthy chieftain."

I merely nod as I keep my eyes fixed on him.

"The desert is washed clean from your feet. Welcome to the tents of Ishmael of Paran. Soon, we will share warm bread baked this morning with cheese from our goats. Now, tell me who you are, where you come from, and the purpose of your journey."

"I have come here from Canaan to claim that which I lost long ago."

Ishmael's Narrative

"Are you trying to make me laugh? We are traders, and we are known to rob caravans when we deem it necessary. Anything of yours that came to our hands is long sold or traded. What could you possibly claim here?"

"You, my brother, Ishmael. I am Isaac, son of Abraham, your father. Just as you have inhabited my dreams for so many years, I want you in my life as my true brother."

I hardly finish stating my purpose when an elderly woman enters the tent carrying a tray of bread, cheese, and dates. As our eyes meet, she stands momentarily as though turned to stone. Then she whispered to herself as though in a daze, "By the Living One Who Sees Me, this is Isaac, son of Abraham. The master's eyes look out from your eyes, and your mouth and chin are those of Abraham."

"Mother," said Ishmael, "please put the food down before you faint, and let me speak with Isaac."

Ishmael's mother, Hagar, quickly leaves the tent empty-handed but burdened with worry. She can justly wonder what indignity or cruel act the son of Sarah might have come to perform in their camp. Her hair is entirely gray, and her skin looks like leather from years of living in a wilderness that has constantly demanded that she yield her moisture. Despite the passage of years and Paran's heat, traces of an enticing beauty remain in Hagar. This woman was always a presence in Abraham's heart, so much so that years after he banished her and her son, he continued to speak of her.

"Mother is shocked by your coming here."

"What about you, Ishmael?"

"For a great many years, I have thought you might seek me out. It was on your account that Father banished Mother and me from his tents in Canaan. Now you come seeking me as a brother. Truly, as noble as is your purpose, that goal may prove quite unlikely."

"Ishmael, I want to build a bond of brotherhood with you. When our tie was severed because of decisions made by our parents, we were neither considered nor consulted."

"That is true, Isaac, but I have lived long and well without you, brother. That life was another time and place in the painful landscape of my childhood. Why do I need you now?"

Ishmael is silent, and I do not hurry to answer him. At this moment, Eliezer, I wish I had consulted you about this journey of seeking. All I can think of is how you have always listened with your heart. It seems to me that is what I can do for my brother, Ishmael.

"I cannot exactly answer why you need me, Ishmael. I can tell you I need you because ever since you were driven out after my weaning, my life has felt broken. It is as though I am a clay pot with a shard missing from its side. I am looking for wholeness, which can come only from our renewed brotherhood."

"Isaac, just as Abraham let me go, and, with one or two ancient exceptions, has not sought me out, why can't you let me be? If I can put the past behind bolted doors, I think you must do the same."

"I cannot because of my Covenant with El Shaddai."

"I am not grasping your meaning. Father used to teach us that recognizing the uniqueness and oneness of El Shaddai, to be wholehearted with Him, was what the Covenant required of us. What does that have to do with your journey to me?"

"My brother, my understanding of the Covenant with El Shaddai is different than Abraham's. To me, being wholehearted with El Shaddai is possible only by being united with the hearts of other people. I know of no more immediate and close place to start than with you, Ishmael."

"I think you have misread El Shaddai's Covenantal arrangement, Isaac. How can a God who demands the rejection and exile of a firstborn son ask you to pursue wholeness? The El Shaddai whose faith we sucked from Abraham's breast is, in reality, a faithless deceiver, a destroyer of family unity, capricious and unjust. Don't speak to me of El Shaddai's Covenant."

"Father's God is not entirely my God. I have learned. I have gone beyond what we were taught. I have found a path in life."

Ishmael's Narrative

"I, too, learned along the way. Let me tell you what I have come to understand since the day Mother and I were banished from Abraham's camp."

Ishmael half closes his eyes as though gazing back toward a distant route he had long ago traversed. He takes a deep breath and waits a few moments before he continues. I do not break the silence. In those minutes without speech, I consider my brother's name. Ishma-el means God will hear. Again, I realize that the greatest gift, the most godly act I can do for my brother, is to listen. I will offer my presence, my concentration, my ears, and my heart, just as Eliezer has done for me over the many years of my need. Would receiving his story bring us nearer to one another in a brotherly bond?

Ishamael continues, "It was just a few days following the thirteenth year of my birth that Father came to me and led me by the arm under a tamarisk tree. He wanted to speak privately and confidentially to me. His summons made me feel truly like the adult the number of my years bespoke. What gave me concern was the look of another world that Father wore.

"'Ishmael, my son, we have been privileged to receive a word of renewed promise from El Shaddai. Last night, He spoke to me and promised progeny and patrimony. This land will be ours forever and will be filled with my offspring and their numerous descendants. Indeed, El Shaddai's message hardly needed to be spoken to me because I have long considered your birth to be the beginning of the fulfillment of the Covenant of El Shaddai.'

"I started to answer Father with words that affirmed my own commitment to El Shaddai, but he held up his hand to silence me.

"'There was more in El Shaddai's message, Ishmael. You know that this Covenant promises boundless reward, but it also makes daunting demands, not the least of which is to walk a different path from our neighbors. In our hearts, we set ourselves apart, and we are set apart through El Shaddai's Covenant.'

"I told Father, 'I am aware of this path, distinct from the Canaanite path, that El Shaddai requires of us. To this path, I am ready to give myself.'

"Father nodded thoughtfully and said, 'We will see. We will see if you can meet El Shaddai's test.'

"'What test are you speaking of?' I asked Father. 'Have I not heeded El Shaddai's words as you have taught them?'

"'El Shaddai has summoned us,' said Father, 'not only to keep our distinct path in our hearts. He charges us now to mark our flesh with a sign of our distinction. El Shaddai bids us remove the flesh of our foreskins this very day. This is not a charge solely to us but to all of our males, descendants and slaves alike.'

"I hardly understood what Father was saying. Questions rushed from me. 'What does this mean, Father? How will we do this thing? Does El Shaddai really want us to go through such pain? Forgive me, Father, but are you certain El Shaddai asks this?'

"Father's eyes flashed a flaming anger. He said, 'I do not doubt El Shaddai's command, and neither must you. Our Covenant is meant to be a Covenant of the flesh. Watch and learn what trust in El Shaddai brings forth!'

"Father pulled a flint knife from his robe. He hoisted up the hem of his robe over his waist, thus revealing himself. He took his foreskin between his thumb and forefinger, pinching and stretching it as far forward as he could. Without hesitation, he sliced through it with the knife. He neither winced nor cried out. He held his severed foreskin up, arm extended toward heaven, and whispered, 'El Shaddai, through my blood, this blood of the Covenant, may my offspring live and grow numerous.'

"I said to myself, the only way this old man could accomplish such a feat was if he were drugged with laudanum. Clearly, he was not. He was benumbed with his intense conviction about the will of El Shaddai. I knew I was not so benumbed, nor so entranced by the divine command.

"'Father, this command is beyond me,' I said. He was wrapping himself to staunch his bleeding.

"'Ishmael, this is a sacrifice you must make, a sacrifice of yourself to El Shaddai. There is no choice about entering the Covenant of the flesh. The only choice you have is to remove your foreskin as I have done or to have Eliezer use his knife while servants hold you.'

"I began to perspire and to feel nauseated. For my whole life up to now, I had always tried to please Father through the most careful obedience. I knew of no other way to act against Sarah's ill will toward me and my mother. Now Father was requiring me to shed my blood in pain and in silence, and I did not know if I could fulfill his demand. Something in me kept wondering whether El Shaddai could require such bloodletting and agony as a statement of loyalty. I had worked hard to create friendships among the Canaanite youth. I could hear in my mind their laughter and derision as soon as they would see me when we bathe at the springs. 'Why is it not enough for El Shaddai that I remain different in my heart? Does He need me to be distinguished in my flesh as well?' At that moment, I considered running from the camp to disappear among the towns of the Canaanites.

"Father saw my rising panic and trembling. He came forward. He wiped my forehead and hugged me close to him. Then, I knew if I were to keep his love, I must submit to the outrageous demand of El Shaddai.

"'Let Eliezer wield the knife while servants hold me,' I said.

"That is what occurred, Isaac. Eliezer worked quickly, and the servants held me firmly. Suddenly there was crushing pressure and a searing flame in my groin the likes of which I had not known before or since, doused only by the blackness of my fainting. Before that blessed night descended on me, I felt a prideful comfort in realizing I had neither wept nor cried out. When I came back to full consciousness, Eliezer gave me a cloth to keep the bleeding in check. Now I was certain that what I had agreed to undergo was for Father's sake, not for El Shaddai. Why would the God of the universe make such a demand on me or on anyone else? Father believed he was so commanded, and I yielded. But, Isaac, I resolved not to put my sons through such a sacrifice. All twelve of my sons, here in Paran, remain completely whole."

I never take my eyes off Ishmael as he speaks. I listen to him intently. I let silence reign for a time before I speak.

"Ishmael, I cannot imagine your pain and fright. It must have shattered your heart that Father put you through such agony."

"You are correct, Isaac. Father removed your foreskin when you were eight days old. You cannot remember being a sacrifice to Father's El Shaddai madness. At least he came to his senses enough to discover that El Shaddai prefers smaller and more tender foreskins. Your future offspring will not know the horror of what I experienced."

"No, Ishmael, they will not. I am amazed at your loyalty to El Shaddai after what you experienced."

"Oh, my brother, you are making a large assumption. Do you imagine that El Shaddai is still my God or that the Covenant between us lives? No, Isaac, I am free of El Shaddai as well as of his unceasing demands, which exceed all boundaries."

I must have blanched when I heard Ishmael's words, because he said to me, "Do not think that my break with El Shaddai is only about foreskins. There is more—a great deal more, with pain that surpassed even that of circumcision. Can you hear it, brother? Are you prepared to listen further?"

"I am here, Ishmael."

"On the day of your birth, I was so happy to have a brother that I laughed and ran about the camp with wild joy. Even though there were many years between us, I looked to the day when I would teach you the skills of the bow. The thought of exploring the hill country with you and introducing you to Canaanite friends was a dream I could hardly wait to realize.

"My elation lasted but a few days. When you were entered into the Covenant of the flesh on the eighth day of your life, I was not present to watch. I certainly would not celebrate what I could not bear to remember undergoing months earlier. As you were brought into Father's tent on a bed of sheep skins, I fled to be invisible to Father. He rarely spoke to me after that and never sought me out. I felt like a shadow hovering about the camp where once I had been a prince.

"Yet, I could not keep away from you, my brother. At every opportunity, I would come to you to make faces, and you laughed and gurgled. Of course, I could only entertain you when Sarah was not holding you. When she put you on skins for a nap under the shady oak, I came to you to play and to tease. One day, as I looked into your eyes as you lay on your back, Sarah hurried over, waving me away with a cloth in her hand.

"'Go, get away from the child. I don't want your shadow upon him. Go, you wild ass!'

"That was the first of numerous times your mother would call me a wild ass. She kept me away from you. Rarely were you out of her sight. It was as though you were lost to me, and I was cut off and buried like my foreskin. And every time she would call me a wild ass, I wanted to tear down her tent and all of the camp. If my name is to be 'Wild Ass,' I thought, my deeds should reflect my name. The more invisible I felt, the more of a wild ass I became.

"Father came to me and said, 'Ishmael, my son, I beg you not to anger Sarah. Cease your antics and your taunting, and all will be well.' He quickly walked away from me, but he had called me 'my son.' Such words were a balm, a poultice to my wounded self. I vowed not to be so loud and playful—even to become more invisible—if that was the coin to purchase Father's love.

"For a time, I managed my impulses. My sadness at being kept from you and at Father's distance actually aided me in becoming invisible. I would leave for days at a time to hunt and practice my archery. Little else but these excursions succeeded in lifting the weight from my spirit. In camp, my days were silent and dark. Then, after a time, I would encounter Father. He would say, 'I see an ill spirit is on you, my son. Perhaps you should go out to the fields.' His words were laden with concern for me. I detected a yearning in him to reach out to me, which I knew Sarah had shackled. While there was a hidden tenderness in his words, his suggestion that I leave camp felt like a small expulsion.

"Two years passed, and I felt myself shrinking in my own eyes to a speck of dust. The goats and camels seemed more valued than me, who bore the mark of El Shaddai's Covenant in my flesh. As the time of your weaning feast drew near, I could not stand my situation any longer. Sarah ordered my mother around in a tone more harsh than one would use on a mongrel dog. At night, I would hear Mother sobbing in her tent because Father ceased to be a husband to her. I knew all of this was a result of your birth, which, instead of fulfilling Sarah, made her a lioness on your behalf. How often I saw the way Father looked at Hagar with desire, but dared not cross Sarah. I did not know what to do, but I felt that a fire was about to break forth.

"The night of your weaning feast came. Hundreds of Canaanite men of renown and their families streamed into our camp. I was now fifteen—a man. Yet I was not invited into the men's circle with the chieftains. From the edge of the circle, I stood looking on as you were presented. Everyone started to clap and whistle. Women chirped and trilled their tongues, except for Hagar, alone in her tent.

"At that moment, a spirit seized me to end my invisibility. I ran from the edge of the camp to where you stood, receiving adulation. I swept you up and put you on my shoulders. I ran toward the fields while you giggled and laughed, tugging at my hair. When we reached the field, I took you down. I knew all eyes in the camp were on us. The look of panic on Sarah's face as I ran with you was pressed into my mind. I decided to give everyone in that assembly a memory to take with them.

"As you stood near the field, I backed away from you by ten or fifteen cubits. I took an arrow from the quiver and fitted it to my bow. I shot that arrow over your head and into the field. I repeated the shot with several more arrows. You stood there smiling and reaching up for the arrows. Even as a two-year-old, you knew I meant no harm. I knew I only intended to show off and shake up the assembly. Sarah and several others ran to us. Your mother grabbed you into her arms. She looked back at me and hissed, 'Wild ass!' I went to my tent. The weaning feast quickly ended with the local greats returning home.

"Sometime later, when the moon was over Philistia to the west, Father came into my tent and shook me. 'Get up, pack your things, and go with Hagar. Sarah insists you leave this camp forever. My son, I can do nothing to change this. Even El Shaddai came to me this night, instructing me to heed Sarah.'

"El Shaddai had once insisted I bear the Covenant in my flesh. Now El Shaddai wanted me to realize my partial invisibility with a total eclipse of myself. Exile, separation, and abandonment were Sarah's demands. El Shaddai was no more willing to oppose her decision than was Abraham. The Covenant, whose mark I bore in my flesh, was shattered for me. Indignity and shame were my legacies.

"Mother was standing outside my tent as I parted the flaps and stood up in the chill of the air. Tears flowed from her eyes, but no words were spoken between us. Father gave her cheese and bread as well as a goat skin of water.

"He stammered, 'This is not my wish, but Sarah's need. El Shaddai has affirmed Sarah's demand. Ishmael, you went too far. El Shaddai will protect you. Go south. I did not intend this. El Shaddai will care for you. Go, go! Go with El Shaddai.'

"As the moon set, we left, heading southward. Father, in his faith-driven obedience, had sacrificed his firstborn son and my mother, the vessel for his superannuated potency. Yes, I say 'sacrificed,' for we did not believe we would survive our exile. I can only think that age sapped the courage Abraham had once displayed against the Canaanite kings or in standing up to El Shaddai for the cities of the plain. We learned as dawn broke how cowardice desolates trust and love."

Ishmael takes a long drink from a gourd. I remain silent, restraining any arguments and listening for further revelations of Ishmael's heart. After some minutes of silence, I ask Ishmael to excuse me so I can go out for some air. I walk around the lush oasis and then beyond into the desert. The scent of creosote and acacia rouses a memory.

V

Moriah: Recurring Nightmare

WHEN ISHMAEL USED THE word "sacrifice" to encompass his bitter treatment at the hands of Abraham and Sarah, my near-sacrifice on Moriah rose before my eyes. It was not merely a recollection. The vision of Moriah is an all-consuming invasion of my being. As Ishmael talked to me, I poured my attention toward his story. Nonetheless, the events around Moriah, a looming mountain of terror, encroached on my ability to concentrate on Ishmael's words. This is what I remember of what I have called the Moriah betrayal.

The sun had not yet risen when Abraham came into my tent, shaking my shoulder with persistence. The sky was beginning to lighten. My heavy slumber also lightened when Father said, "Isaac, my son, get up! We're going on a journey."

His words roused and excited me. I asked him, "Who is going?" He answered, "Just you and me and a couple of the servant boys." I was thrilled at having Father to myself.

"Where are we going, Father?" I asked.

"We will go wherever El Shaddai leads us for three days. Now, hurry and get dressed. I have packed provisions for the journey. Let's not delay El Shaddai's purpose."

I came out of my tent bursting with excitement to go with Father at El Shaddai's bidding. "Father, since we are going away for several days, I want to say goodbye to Mother."

"Your mother was sick all night long. She needs to sleep. She needs to get her strength back. She knows you are coming with me. Her love is going with you."

We set off with the donkey and the two servant lads. In my rush to be ready to set off, I did not notice the bundle of sticks on the donkey's back. Had I paid attention, no doubt I would have thought Father did not want to gather kindling and firewood at the end of each day's journey.

We started walking to the northeast on a path from Be'er Sheva. The journey was not difficult because the terrain was mostly flat with some modest hills. As we walked, questions I had always wanted to ask Father came into my mind. Our lives were so full of tending our flocks, shearing our sheep, and finding fresh grass. I rarely had an opportunity to have a talk with Father. "Father, you mentioned El Shaddai's purpose for our journey. How does El Shaddai speak to you? You say our God has no body. Then without lips, tongue, and mouth, how does Shaddai speak?"

"Isaac, my son, I see you have learned something of the nature of our God. Indeed, El Shaddai has no speech organs, but Shaddai is the source of thought and speech. When El Shaddai speaks to me, it is as though words are written on my heart just as a stylus inscribes a clay tablet. Those words, El Shaddai's instructions, are as clear to me as what my ears tell me when you talk to me."

"Father, what did El Shaddai tell you is the purpose of this journey of three days?"

"Isaac, it is too early to share El Shaddai's purpose with you. You will learn on the third day the holy reason for our walk."

As a boy of thirteen years, I was not too good at waiting or being patient. I knew as well that nagging Father to tell me would be useless. We walked on in silence until the sun was setting. The servants set up our tent. Father ordered them to gather sticks and build a fire for the evening. I thought it odd that with all the sticks our donkey carried, Father told them to collect wood there in the foothills.

"Father, why are you telling the servants to gather sticks when we have brought wood?"

"My son, we are carrying our own wood to use on the third day of our journey. We may not find firewood at our destination."

Our meal around the fire that evening was dried goat meat, onions, olives, bread, and dates. We went into the tent tired and ready for sleep after our long day's walk. We awoke with the first rays of the sun. Father encouraged me to eat well because he said we would be climbing uphill today and tomorrow. He said we were heading toward Yevus, a town nestled among the tops of the hills. Some called it by its other name, Shalem, the place of wholeness. Father said it earned that second name because its inhabitants, who came from different lands with different gods, all learned to live together with mutual respect. Their leader, Melchizedek, was renowned for his generosity and hospitality. I was not yet aware that the town and its tallest peak, Moriah, I would come to think of as Shever, the site of fracture, calamity, and rupture.

We began to climb the mountains of the east away from Canaan's coastal plain and elevate ourselves above and beyond the Negev's parched landscape. We went up slowly, making our way between the pines and oaks and around limestone boulders. Father was spry for his years. I sensed it was the mission from El Shaddai that guided his steps.

"Father." My voice broke his concentration on some distant point.

"I am here for you, my son."

"When will we reach our destination? Are we going to enter Yevus?"

"Isaac, we will get to where we are going by midday tomorrow. We will not enter Yevus. We will ascend the hill to the north of the town. The hill is called Moriah."

"Does El Shaddai live on Moriah, Father?"

"El Shaddai fills every space in the world, but there is an abundant measure of his spirit on Moriah."

"So, are we going to Moriah to draw near to El Shaddai, Father?"

"Yes, my son, we will draw near together."

Moriah: Recurring Nightmare

On the second night of our journey, I did not rest well. My sleep was invaded by a scary dream beyond my understanding. I dreamed of two rams that were running around in panic. Since I spent my days with our flocks back home, dreaming of sheep and goats was not unusual. But, in this dream, suddenly the two rams stopped running and stood in place rigidly as though they were tethered. They turned their faces towards me. They stared with pleading eyes. When I looked at their faces, one was Ishmael's. The other ram had my own face. A ram's horn sounded, and the rams ran off. I woke up trembling from the horror of this dream, whose meaning I did not understand. After a hurried breakfast, we continued our climb.

On the third morning, at one point, Father called a rest stop. He ordered the servants to unpack the saddlebags that were strapped to the donkey. Father explained that he wanted to make sure he had brought the necessary supplies.

The servants placed goat skins on the ground. Upon the skins, they set out the remainder of our food provisions. The last items they took out of the saddlebags were a knife about half a cubit long and a flint stone for sparking a fire. This effort at taking stock of what was in the saddle bags roused my curiosity. After looking at the materials on the ground, Father ordered everything to be put back in the bags, except for the knife and the flint stone.

When the servants had repacked the bags and tied them to the donkey, Father took the bundle of sticks. He took up his knife and the flint stone. Turning to the servants, Father told them, "You stay here with the donkey. Isaac and I will go on to worship El Shaddai and then come back to you." The servants did as they were instructed. Father and I, alone, walked on together.

Like a sudden gust of wind that blows sand and stings the eyes and face, I knew immediately why I could not sleep the last night. Father had said we were to draw near to El Shaddai on Moriah. The word we use for making a sacrifice also means to draw near. Father had taken a special slaughtering knife to slay the lamb. He had the flint stone to create a fire to send up the slain burnt offering to El Shaddai. We were going to perform a sacrifice on

Moriah. Even though I had reached some understanding of what was to take place on Moriah, I was still puzzled. I decided to ask.

"Father!"

"I am here, my son."

"Father, it seems we are going to draw near to El Shaddai by making a sacrifice. I see you have the special knife and the flint stone. Where is the lamb by which we shall draw near to El Shaddai?"

"Isaac, El Shaddai will provide the lamb for the burnt offering."

What did father mean? A lamb for a sacrifice must be taken from one's own herd. It cannot be a wild animal. Neither can it be an animal stolen from a neighbor. Where would father get a lamb on this mountain? I pondered over this puzzle.

We two walked on together.

As I continued on the path with Father on my left, I felt a presence moving with us on my right. I glanced that way. There was no person there, yet the presence of a being was immediate and actual. A shining rippling of the air, much like the light of a desert mirage, accompanied me on my right. If Father noticed, it was not apparent at first.

Just as Father had described to me how he heard El Shaddai not through physical hearing but as words in his heart, that was my experience with the shimmering, transparent presence. As though whispering to me, it spoke with urgency.

"Boy, you are on a mountaintop. There are no lambs up here. The old man has a plan for you, and it is not holy. Run! You can outrun him. Save your life!"

Without speaking aloud, I answered, "We are here at El Shaddai's bidding. No harm will come to me. I am Father's only son by Sarah. I am most beloved and precious to him. Be gone! Intrude your doubts elsewhere. Be gone!"

The shimmering air departed. It reappeared on Father's left. He froze. I could sense the words Father was trying to stave off. "Don't be a pawn for El Shaddai's bidding, Abraham. You earned Isaac by standing up to El Shaddai's daunting tests. Put El Shaddai in his place, as you did when you confronted him in Sodom.

El Shaddai wants to break the Covenant with you by demanding Isaac. What kind of god do you obey? He is no different than the gods Chemosh, Ba'al, or Milcom in his demand for human sacrifice. Spare your son. You cannot live with his destruction."

Father flung his arm toward his left several times, as though shooing away a biting desert fly. I never, in all my life, had reason to disbelieve or not trust Father. Surely his love and his doting on me were more certain than some mountain jinn pursuing mischief, trying to come between me and my father. We continued on the path.

We reached a wooded flat area at the top of Moriah. Father told me to put the sticks on the ground and to gather rocks as heavy as I could carry. He said he would use them to build an altar that needed to stand firm. It took a little time to collect the rocks and for Father to build the altar. He told me to arrange the sticks upon the altar. During this time, no lamb or goat appeared on the mountain.

"Father?"

"I am here, Isaac, my son."

"There is still no lamb for the offering. What shall we do? You said El Shaddai would provide."

Father was sitting on a rock when I spoke to him. He said, "Come here, my son." I approached him and stood close in front of him. He put his hands on my shoulders and looked into my eyes. He had a length of rope at his feet by the side of the rock. He took an end of the cord and began slowly and gently coiling it around me. In a voice hoarse with emotion, almost too soft to hear, he said, "My son, you are the lamb El Shaddai demands. El Shaddai made you a gift to your mother and me. He came to me three days ago to ask me to return you. Just as your arrival to us was a surprise, so His call to return you stuns me. We have no choice but to obey El Shaddai."

I did have a choice. I could have run off the mountain to keep far from my father, who was intoxicated and hypnotized by his faith in El Shaddai. I had to flee and head into the wilderness to save myself. I started to turn from Father, but his hands were still on my shoulders. The cords were firmly around my arms and legs. My mind and heart freed me to run, while the bonds on my legs tripped me. Freedom denied!

Father picked up my bound body and walked to the altar he had built underneath an oak tree. He set me on my back on top of the wood and sticks that were resting on the stones of the sacrificial offering. I could barely breathe in my terror. Words were prisoners in the constricted cell of my throat. My mind kept repeating, "El Shaddai is a liar. Father is a betrayer. Father is a liar. El Shaddai is a betrayer. The Covenant I have heard about all my life is false."

As Father stood beside the altar, preparing to raise the knife over my chest, I stared at the sky through the branches of the oak above me. The sky was cloudless and cerulean. It was not a whole expanse of firmament. The branches of the oak over me seemed to divide the sky into fragments of jagged blue. The sky was shattered. My life was shattered. Truth was razed and trust was rent, just as the heavens over me were broken. I lay upon the altar. My vision blurred as my tears mingled with Father's falling tears. I squeezed my eyes shut so as not to see the plunging knife. I pictured it looming as Father raised the instrument of my death above his head. I waited for the final searing pain that Father's whetted bronze blade would inflict. I awaited the blackness that would follow the ebbing of my blood. I wondered whether my last sound would be like a lamb bleating. The final question that flashed into my mind like a lightning bolt was whether Mother had any idea of Father's murderous betrayal.

Father seemed to hesitate at his task for the briefest moment. I opened my eyes. The sky above me had become a lapis lazuli royal blue and then turned black, with stars scattered in the dark. In one corner of the sky, I saw the crescent new moon with its horns at each end shining light on Father, much like the shimmering presence we had encountered on the trail here.

With that presence of light, my heart heard what I took to be the voice of El Shaddai.

"Abraham, Abraham!"

"I am here, El Shaddai!"

Moriah: Recurring Nightmare

"Do not lay your hand upon the lad, for now I know you revere me!"

Father dropped the knife, lowered his hand, and moved away from the altar. I saw him look up and start heading toward a thicket. The sky became as bright as noonday again. As though the oak branches had disappeared, the sky was an expanse of blue. From the direction that Father went, I could hear the sound of a trapped ram. As Father chased the ram, I wriggled off the altar, freeing myself of the restricting cord. I ran in the opposite direction from where Father had gone.

I could not meet Father and accompany him home. I did not think I could ever look at him or speak to him again. My life had been spared, but my love and trust were shattered on the sacrificial altar. My spirit was wounded; it was beyond healing, I thought.

Now, I rouse myself from this nightmare, which has frequently visited my life. I retrace my steps over the gravel of Wadi Paran. I head back to Ishmael's tent at the oasis. Now I must resume being an audience for his story. I want to receive his words, his narrative. I am already aware of the slightest movement toward me by Ishmael. Now that I have remembered yet again the Moriah betrayal, I can hear Ishmael in the present. We will talk about the past and, I hope, create a future of brotherhood together.

VI

Twin Tales

I COME BACK TO Ishmael's tent. He is not there. His mother, Hagar, meets me. She tells me to wait for him while he finishes trading with a Midianite caravan.

"I am grateful, Isaac, to have a few minutes alone with you. You need to know that when Abraham expelled us from the camp, it was more than exile. It exceeded betrayal. His love seemed to vanish like morning fog.

"I say 'his love' because I have complete certainty that Abraham loved Ishmael and me intensely. Even before Sarah allowed me to be her surrogate to produce a child with Abraham, he and I shared an attraction that become a bond. When Sarah grudgingly allowed Abraham to enter my tent, he did so without hesitation. He masked his enthusiasm. In the tent, he was gentle and loving to me. He whispered how he would fill me with his seed, that I would give him a son. Inside me, his ardor was like that of a young man. I was lifted to the clouds not once but several times.

"I conceived Ishmael that night. Sarah never permitted Abraham to approach me again. I knew whenever Abraham's gaze met mine that our attraction and yearning remained alive. As for Ishmael, it was clear how deeply his father loved him. Abraham took Ishmael frequently to show him his flocks and herds. He made sure that his servants and retainers were familiar to Ishmael.

As Ishmael grew up, he taught the boy about El Shaddai and the Covenant. More than once, I heard Abraham softly murmur a prayer, asking that Ishmael be accepted to walk with El Shaddai as a Covenant partner. It would have been sufficient for Abraham to have Ishmael be his successor as a prince in Canaan and a vassal of El Shaddai.

"None of this would come to pass once El Shaddai opened Sarah's womb. She conceived and bore you, Isaac. Then, our presence in the camp vexed her beyond toleration. She determined that Ishmael and I leave the camp. Abraham came to me the night before our expulsion to tell me that Sarah and El Shaddai insisted on our departure. At that moment, it became clear to me that Abraham was offering Ishmael and me as a sacrifice by driving us into the wilderness.

"In reality, Abraham and Sarah placed an order of execution on us. He sent us into the wilderness with a bit of bread and cheese, barely enough for a day and a night. He gave us a goat skin of water, too small to last in the fiery kiln of the desert in summer. Yet it was heavy. We dragged it with a rope through gravel and sand. It left a track that could lead some desert travelers to our vulture-picked corpses.

"After three days, we had consumed our food and water. We were in the Wilderness of Paran, the wild place. Your brother, Ishmael, was depleted, unable to walk further. I was drained of energy. My spirit was an empty cistern. There was no water of hope within me. I helped Ishmael to the meager shade of a broom tree. There he lay delirious. I moved away from him. I could not release him from his pain and groaning. I did not wish to witness the agony of his death.

"There was a clump of bushes nearby. I had not noticed it initially. As I lay in the gravel, I heard a faint, gurgling trickle of water. At first, I was sure I was hallucinating. The sound awakened a dawning of hope in me. I had a flashing vision of Ishmael as a man of great strength, a father of many children, and a leader among tribes. That image gave me strength to get up. I went to the clump of bushes. A modest, gently flowing spring of water revealed itself. I let the water flow into the goat skin, drank a few swallows, and brought the water to Ishmael. Soon he revived. He got up. We remained at this flowing, sustaining spring. What you see before you at this oasis is the spring and pool we dug out. We call it Be'er Lachai Ro'i, the Well of the Living One Who Sees Me. Here we encountered Chai, the Living One, our God and protector."

Hagar's story shakes me like trembling ground beneath my feet. I feel a pain, a pressure, in my entire back, like what I felt atop the wood on the altar on Moriah. As I catch my breath, I ask her if Chai is another name for El Shaddai, Abraham's God.

She says, "Isaac, El Shaddai is a name that means 'sufficient.' El Shaddai refers to the idea that God is sufficient. Was Shaddai sufficient for the unguided and morally ignorant people of Sodom, victims of the raining brimstone? Was Shaddai sufficient when he demanded the blood and flesh of Abraham's and Ishmael's foreskins as a Covenantal tribute? El Shaddai was not sufficient when Abraham drove us from his tents. The God we met here in Paran at this spring is life. Our God saved our lives, protected and sustained us. Chai gave us life. Chai made no demands on us other than to protect and sustain one another in our clan. More than this Chai does not require, and Chai's living waters keep flowing, feeding us and our flocks and date palms."

"Praise Chai, praise Chai," says Ishmael as he enters the tent with confident strides. "Those Midianites were so eager to trade for our speckled sheep skins that they were generous in paying with gold, aloe balm, and laudanum. Now we have added not only to our wealth but also to our capacity to heal and be healed."

"Brother," I say, "we have more yet to heal us beside what you got from the traders of Midian. It seems we have both been sacrifices by Abraham to El Shaddai."

"What are you talking about, Isaac? No one else among the tents of Abraham was abused as Mother and I were by Father's fanaticism. My imposed circumcision as a young man. Our exile from the camp. We were living sacrifices pushed to the edge of extinction. How can you, a pampered shepherd prince, dare to see yourself as a sacrifice? You were an eight-day-old infant, oblivious to your circumcision. You lost your elder brother when you were but a toddler. Where is the sacrifice in any of your past? It is really laughable that you compare your life to mine."

"Ishmael, I came to Paran to tell you I recognize and honor your strength. I acknowledge your suffering at the hand of Abraham. I celebrate your achievements—that you are the father of twelve children and a mighty chieftain. But, even though my birth was the reason for your exile, it was Sarah's jealousy and Father's fanaticism that led to your near-sacrifice. As for me, I idolized you. I would have gladly yielded to you my status in the family and my Covenant with El Shaddai."

"I know, Isaac, in the depths of my heart, that you were not responsible for what Abraham did. I suppose it was not really a surprise when Father approached Mother and me with cheese, the goat skin of water, and his verbal shove of the two of us toward the south. I had heard every day for several years the way Sarah spoke to my mother. No matter the effort Mother made or the haste and care with which she waited upon her, Sarah was a harsh and critical mistress. Her tongue was a slashing whip. Her words were a scorpion sting on Mother's spirit. Our father stood by, averted his eyes, or retreated into his tent. He never tried to calm Sarah's cruel jealousy.

"There is one other strange happening that was part of our expulsion from the camp. What I am going to tell you I have not told even my mother. I had a delirious dream two nights after Abraham banished Mother and me. Father comes into my tent and shakes me out of my sleep. He tells me to dress for a three-day journey. I ask where we are going. He tells me we are going to the Far Place, the site where our descendants would build a noble sanctuary.

"I am so excited to go on this journey with Father. I hurry to get ready. We walk and we walk. Father is distant. He does not talk to me. Something is occupying his thoughts. I ask him what the purpose of our journey is. He looks at me directly and says, 'El Shaddai demands you as a sacrifice on the mountain.' I shove him away from me. I run. I take flight like a desert vulture. I nest in a cliff I do not recognize. Mother rouses me, pouring water on my face and into my mouth. I awaken. I am shaking. This dream of mine is an omen of a future that I cannot discern. I did come to understand that what we endured in our exile, Mother and I, was Abraham's sacrifice."

Though Ishmael is a mighty chieftain and the father of twelve tribes, tears run down his cheeks. I sense how vivid and excruciatingly fresh to him was his treatment by our father. Ishmael reaches for a small jug of goat milk to calm and refresh himself.

"Ishmael, I need to tell you that what you dreamed, I myself experienced at Abraham's hand. I lived that nightmare. Our father did lead me up to the mountain called Moriah, near Yevus. There he literally tied me to a stone altar, binding me with rope and with the coils of deceit. I can still feel the wood on which he placed me digging into my back. Father raised the slaughtering knife. I feared the pain of the plunging knife and the blackness of death. Yet, I felt in a corner of my soul relief at being released from El Shaddai's Covenant and Father's unrestrained obedience to it. But his knife never pierced my breast. Suddenly, he suspended his arm and dropped the knife. We heard the bleating of a nearby ram. Father ran off to find it for a replacement sacrifice. I freed myself from that altar and ran in the direction opposite from Father, toward the town of Yevus."

"So, Isaac, what are you doing here? Does not seeing me and hearing my story revive dormant pain? I know that is how I feel about your appearance at this oasis. It's a wonder you could return to his tents after what you saw of his religious fanaticism and deception. Did I tell you that he has come by this oasis twice to check up on me? I always avoid his visits. I do not plan to encounter him again."

"Penetrating questions, my brother Ishmael, demand honest answers. I could not have returned to the tents of Abraham any more than you could, were it not for the wisdom of one who was compassionate and able to read my heart. As I said, I ran from the heights of Moriah down to the city of Yevus. People quickly saw that I was a stranger. Word spread that an unknown lad ran alone into the city. When the news of my arrival reached the king, whose name is Melchizedek, he summoned me to his court. I was escorted to him by two of his officers.

"The king asked, 'Who are you, lad, and why did you come running into our city? Reports tell me you came in rushing like a desert jinn.'

"'I was running from my father, who tied me to an altar on Moriah to sacrifice me to his God.'

"'Your Canaanite dialect tells me you have come here perhaps from the Negev, from Arad, or from Be'er Sheva. Why did your father bring you to this land?'

"'He claimed that his God, El Shaddai, so commanded him.'

"'El Shaddai? Here we worship El Elyon, the Most High God. I am his priest as well as the king. There is only one person I have ever heard speak of El Shaddai. That is Abraham of Haran, who moved with his family to Canaan several decades ago. Is it too much to imagine that you are a son of his?'

"'No, Highness, you are correct. I am the son of Abraham, and my mother is Sarah. I was not born to them until they were in their nineties. All was well until three days ago, when Father took the notion to offer me to El Shaddai as a sacrifice. He almost succeeded. At the last moment, he dropped his knife to replace me with a ram caught in a nearby thicket. When he hurried to the ram, I ran here to Yevus. Please do not send me back to Father's camp.'"

Ishamel asks me to tell him more about King Melchizedek of Yevus.

VII

The School of Sham V'Avar

"Melchizedek listened to my experience with an intense yet calm countenance. He remained silent for several moments. Then he looked into my eyes as though searching a pool for a tiny fish. He spoke softly to me. The king said, 'You have had a shattering occurrence at your father's hand.' He seemed to sense what I felt when he said, 'Your soul feels fragmented like a smashed jug.'

"'That is just how I feel,' I said. 'Shards. My soul is in pieces. I am lost and angry. I am betrayed and frightened. I am detached from everything I thought I understood and believed. I do not see myself healing or reconciling with my father.'

"'Isaac, you called this city Yevus. Many refer to it as you did because our people here are known in Canaan as Yevusim. But I call our city Shalem—the place of wholeness, of renewal, and of reconciliation. Here, if you would remain with me in my home for a time, I think you will find healing and wholeness. There is a spirit in our hills and valleys, a pine-scented breeze of rebirth. It gives many people hope. It enables us to sing and to pour out poetry into the mountain air. The gentle spirit of Ir Shalem, the City of Wholeness, can bring you healing. Stay with me here until you feel your soul repaired.'

"'I answered Melchizedek first with a question. 'O King, you called me Isaac. How did you know my name?'

The School of Sham V'Avar

"'Melchizedek replied, 'Once I realized you were Abraham's son, I knew your name, Isaac. I, along with the other princes of Canaan, attended your weaning ceremony when you were presented to us nearly twelve years ago. And may I say it was quite a party. Your father spared no expense to impress us—as though we were not already in awe of this ninety-year-old who had fathered a son! So, I welcome you, Isaac, into my home. You and your children in a future time will always be welcome in Ir Shalem.'

"I was already feeling a connection to Melchizedek, drawn by his kindness and care for me. That he had known me for most of my life helped bring me near to him. I accepted his offer to live in his house of cool limestone walls for an indeterminate period of time.

"'Isaac, I want to begin by sharing with you the goal and path of your healing. I call it Sham V'Avar, there and past. That is the goal to aim for, to absorb into your soul that what you experienced was in another place and in a past time. If you are able to do so, you will rid yourself of your obsession with the horrible events that befell you. You will no longer feel like shards stuck among the rubble of a garbage heap. You will go forward, whole, focusing on your present and future. Now come with me.'

"Melchizedek led me to a hallway. At its far end was a door of pine. He opened the door with one hand, and in the other, he took up a lighted torch. The doorway brought us to smooth stone stairs leading downward. We descended thirty-six stairs with torches on the wall every six cubits to guide us. Melchizedek lit each torch. The last stair was slightly wider. From there, I could see the light of the nearest torches reflected on flowing water.

"'This is the pool of Shiloach,' said the king. 'Its waters flow from a larger pool south of Shalem. Immerse yourself in these waters of Shiloach. They will wash from you the dust of the road you walked from Be'er Sheva to Moriah. These waters will remove from you the stink of the ass. Just as the ass was innocent and obedient on the journey, so were you. The odor of the same trusting innocence on your part is of putrefying shame to you. That shame turns into the choking, acrid stench of betrayal and victimhood.

Yes, Isaac, immerse yourself in Shiloach's waters. Wash away the encrusted horrors of the recent past, of Moriah. They are over, and you are beyond them.'

"I did immerse as Melchizedek invited me. I peeled off my filthy clothes and dunked myself in the cool waters repeatedly. With each immersion, I felt clean, cool, and relaxed. Then, I remained in the pool, holding my knees to my chest with my face in the water. For a moment, it was as though I didn't exist. Standing up to breathe felt like what I imagine as a first breath at birth. In a small way, I felt a glimmer of renewal, at least cleansed.

"Melchizedek brought me a shirt and pants of linen. After a lifetime of wearing sheep skin and leather, I felt like royalty in the linen garments. Just as the waters of Shiloach cooled me and soothed my spirit, so too did the linen on my skin. Melchizedek led me upstairs from the pool. I followed him to an airy chamber, which had goose down pillows embroidered with colorful designs placed against one wall. The other three walls had protrusions of limestone ledges of different heights. Glass balls, vases, amphoras, and bottles rested on the ledges. The skylight in the ceiling shone sunshine on the glass objects, coaxing out their red, blue, orange, and green colors. They contrasted with the beige-white limestone on which they rested. Melchizedek led me to the pile of pillows. He invited me to sit and told me to spend an hour alone there.

"I nestled on the pillows. I sat quietly and absorbed the variegation and richness of the colors of the glass items. Their glow captured my mind. The colors guided my thoughts to my own inner life. When I gazed at the green balls and disks, I felt strong in body as befitted my fourteen years. In time, the green glow would help me overcome my sense of victimhood and powerlessness.

"The red and orange brightness of the amphoras and vases roused my passion. Eventually I would understand that the passion I felt had many aspects: the desire for a wife, a yearning to be a father on my own terms, different from Abraham, and a passion to root myself in the soil of Canaan.

"The blue color that the glass objects reflected touched a chord deeper and possibly more obscure in my soul. It whispered to me of gentleness and a yearning for connection. It hinted at a hunger I had for truth and wholeness. These feelings I describe to you during my first hour in the stone chamber were vague and not yet defined. I would spend many hours over the next year in meditation on the impact of the colored glass and the sunshine on me.

"When Melchizedek came in after about an hour, he told me that I needed to do one more thing. I was open to his guidance. He showed me to my sleeping chamber. There were mats on the stone floor and two chairs at a table in one corner. He motioned for me to sit. Then he said something that terrified me.

"'I am going to bind your arms with coils of rope, and I will blindfold you with swaths of wool and linen.'

"My heart turned to a rigid lump when I heard Melchizedek. I started to get up from my chair when I saw coils in the king's hands. He reached out to calm me.

"'Isaac, I know how frightening being tied up in these coils seems to you, but I am asking you to trust me further. I will bind your arms tightly to your body. You will unbind yourself as you did on Moriah. In time you will become, in your mind and in your soul, Isaac unbound. The covering on your eyes is to blind you from any distractions. It will help you attend to removing the coils and remember each day's impressions and lessons. In your time of blindness, you will discover some truths.'

"I allowed Melchizedek to bind me and to blindfold me for a time. When I succeeded in unbinding the ropes around my body by twisting my wrists and my shoulders, Melchizedek entered the room. He removed my eye sheath.

"'What did you learn from being sightless?' Melchizedek asked. I said, 'I had a flash, just a brief memory of something I had paid little attention to previously. On the third day of the journey to Moriah, Father told our servants to stay put while he and I would go a distance to worship. Then Father told the servants that, afterward, we would return to them at that place. That memory shocked me because I hadn't heard him tell the servants we would return—or so I thought.'

"'What did the sliver of fleeting recollection tell you, Isaac?'

"'I'm not sure if what Father said was meant to deceive me further or if he believed we'd both come down the mountain. I need to consider this memory and its possible meaning.'

"'Yes, Isaac, I agree that you need to reflect on it. There is much to remember and think about. That's why I invited you to stay here until all is clear and things are where they belong, sham v'avar. Now, go rest. You've had an emotional day. I will come to your bed chamber in two hours to share with you the evening meal.'

"The sun was making its way toward its couch in the Great Sea. As its rays began to disappear, Melchizedek entered the chamber. He was carrying a large ceramic pot painted with leaping gazelles and entwined grape leaves. He set the pot on a floor mat and took two bowls and spoons from under his robe. The smell coming from the pot was one I shall never forget, like a dish cooked just this side of Eden. It had garlic and leeks, lemon, and pungent herbs.

"'This,' said Melchizedek, 'is Judean Hills gazelle stew. No meat is more tender or intensely flavorful. That is because the gazelles eat only the youngest, freshest shoots of grass that surround the oases west of here. No meat, as far as I know, will ever do more to restore your strength. That is why we two will feast on gazelle stew on the eve of the seventh day each week.'

"Eating the stew was so filling and fulfilling. I had never tasted or enjoyed any dish so much. I knew it would be difficult for me to wait until the eve of the seventh day the next week to sup again on that glorious stew. It was one of those rare delicacies that I knew there and then I would always love.

"The day I have described in Melchizedek's palace and under his care became my daily routine: bathing in the waters of Shiloach, meditating in the chamber of glass, and being bound and blinded for an hour. I remained under his tutelage and adhered to the regimen I have described for a year. I was approaching the fifteenth anniversary of my birth. At that time, Melchizedek asked me, 'Isaac, you shared with me your memory of your father telling the servants that the two of you would return to them. As a result of your practice here, how have you come to understand what your father said?'

"'I realized that Father had no need to lie to or deceive the servants. They were his property. He owed them no explanations. He did not need to say those words to distract me, for he knew he had my full allegiance. I have concluded that Father actually believed his words. He was certain El Shaddai wanted his teaching by example, not through the flesh and blood of his son. It has even occurred to me that Father never would have obeyed El Shaddai if he had thought his God was earnest in demanding me as a sacrifice. Father, I think, showed his deep faith in El Shaddai by taking me up the mountain, knowing in the end that my life would not be taken. The excursion to Moriah was Father's way of telling the world that El Shaddai is just and fair. Of course, Father used me to carry forth his teaching. It was shattering and horrific for me. It was unfair, but my life, as I have come to see, was never in danger.'

"Melchizedek asked, 'Then, with this new understanding, can you forgive Abraham? Can you reconcile with him?'

"'I am ready to forgive and to reconcile,' I replied.

"'Then,' said Melchizedek, 'it is time for you to leave Shalem and return to the tents of your father.'

"I bowed before the king. When I stood up, he embraced me and said, 'May El Elyon bless you from our exalted mountain, and may you partake in the well-being of Ir Shalem.'"

VIII

Reconciliation

"These events that you have related to me, Isaac, are almost too much to take in. I have carried for years the feeling that I was a sacrifice made by our father. When I hear what you experienced, it occurs to me that what Father did to my mother and me was not exactly an intentional sacrifice. Yes, he put our lives at risk by exiling us. But, knowing his faith in El Shaddai, I think perhaps he felt certain we would be shielded and sustained by a divine presence in the wilderness. Father's faith was, in the end, justified by my God, Chai Ro'i, the Living One Who Sees Me. Still, when Father threw us out with neither a blessing nor a sympathetic word, it felt like the ultimate betrayal. I cannot forgive him. Now that I've heard your story, I see that his taking you up the mountain felt active and purposeful to you. No, I cannot reconcile with such a fanatic."

"Ishmael, I would not presume to encourage you to forgive Father. His action was beyond what any father could justify. You also did not have the healing experience I had with Melchizedek."

"If you did not come here to persuade me to reconcile with Father, why did you come to my tents and oasis?"

"I will tell you why, Ishmael, but let's walk a bit in your fields. Let's move around."

We leave Ishmael's tent and walk silently towards the fields of wheat and barley that the oasis nurtures. It is late in the afternoon.

RECONCILIATION

Shadows are lengthening, but the field of grain still sends out a golden glow. A subtle breeze bends the stalks of barley and wheat, waving and bowing toward each other. When the light wind ceases for a few minutes, the stalks return to their upright and singular postures.

"You have truly made a wilderness flourish with your irrigation and careful planting."

"Thank you for saying so, Isaac. It is not only because of my family's hard work. Chai Ro'i infuses our fields and orchards with a spark of vitality and renewal. Our God blesses the waters of the oasis and dwells in the reliable sunlight."

"There is something I notice in your field that nourishes me beside its potential to provide bread for all."

"What is that, Isaac?"

"The barley and the wheat grow side by side. They do not compete. The barley was planted earlier than the wheat. The younger wheat bows toward its elder, the barley. The stalks of barley are not too proud to bend to the wheat. Of course, the wind makes them bow, but that, to me, is a symbol of their mutual good will. You are the barley, Ishmael. I am the wheat. The wind is our desire for brotherhood restored."

"Isaac, I have come to see that you are a person of generosity and grand spirit. I am sure I will remain that wild ass of a man the angel described to my mother before my birth. I know I am as rough and abrasive as the gravel of this wilderness. But I see now that I need a brother. Though Abraham exiled my mother and me when you were a toddler, I want you as my brother."

"I, too, have needed you, Ishmael, all my life. Even before I began my search for you in this wilderness, I remembered you and wondered about you frequently."

"I hope you will come to this oasis at Paran to visit me each year for as long as you like."

"You may depend that I will, Ishmael. Now, I have a request of you as well."

"What is it, Isaac? I would gladly do whatever you need."

"When Father dies, I would like you to join me in placing him in his burial cave at Machpelah. I will especially need you by my side."

"Isaac, if you are asking me to be a dutiful son and brother, I will do it for your sake and for our brotherhood. I still will not consider my presence a reconciliation with him, not even at his death."

"Indeed, you may not think of it as a reconciliation, but it will be a moment of letting go of what was. We can't move on alone. I am ready to travel with you beyond anger and abandonment to a place unencumbered by such memories."

"What of your mother, Sarah? Would she tolerate my presence at Abraham's burial? I think my feelings toward her are harsher than those I have toward Father. She was jealous of Hagar and zealous for your position. These things drove her, without any justice, to push Abraham to get rid of Mother and me. I cannot imagine any way that I could stand with you at Father's grave in Sarah's presence. It is beyond my capacity to be there. The very thought of being there with Sarah reduces me to childhood and nearly transforms me into a pillar of salt."

"Ishmael, after this time with you, you can be sure I would never pain you by asking you to be in my mother's presence. Sarah died just a few months after my return from Yevus. She had been aware of Abraham's plan to take me to the place of sacrifice. She was firm in her faith that El Shaddai would protect me. When I did not return to Be'er Sheva with Father, she was certain he had gone through with the deed. Father tried to reassure her that the sacrifice never occurred. These were empty words to her because Father knew neither where I was after he chased the ram nor whether I would return. During the year I spent with Melchizedek in Ir Shalem, Mother took sick with sorrow and mourning. Abraham tried to comfort and strengthen her. She was so deeply angry at Abraham that she took her servant and moved to Kiryat Arba. She weakened with each day of my absence. Two days before I arrived at camp, she returned her spirit to El Shaddai. I will never know whether my presence would have revived her if I had come back earlier. Our faithful servant, Eliezer, led Abraham and the family

RECONCILIATION

to Kiryat Arba. He performed the ceremony of entombment at the cave of Machpelah. He took upon himself the task of shattering her jug as is the custom."

"Isaac, I not only weep for your loss, but I can see more clearly that you were Sarah's whole world. Please believe me when I tell you I know how great her loss of you was. That is how my mother felt here in Paran when I was dying in the heat of the parched ground under a broom tree. I pray that Chai Ro'i and El Shaddai will comfort you for the loss of your mother. Sarah was a devoted mother and a faithful wife. She was royal in her bearing."

"Thank you, my brother, for your words, which enter my heart. Thank you for listening, for your understanding, and for your compassion." This wild ass of a man had transformed himself into a prince of Paran, growing himself into a model of desert expansiveness.

"Isaac, I will always come to you whenever you need me."

"Ishmael, your words are a blessing to me, as is your flourishing oasis. I could remain with you many more months. It is, though, time for me to return to Be'er Sheva. Father sent Eliezer back to Haran to find a wife for me. It would not do to keep a lady waiting who is willing to be my wife sight unseen. I admit I am nervous and, even more, curious. In order to begin to catch up to the grandeur of your family, all my nieces and nephews, I need to get busy with a fertile and willing wife. I can barely stand the wait."

"I understand, brother. I remember that hunger. Go in peace under the watchful gaze of Chai Ro'i."

Ishmael and I hug for a long time. I feel as though his countenance is the face of El Shaddai or Chai Ro'i. That is the sense of wholeness and shalom that renewed brotherhood brings. I mount my ass, which Ishmael loaded with bags of food for my return journey. In three days, I will be home again to encounter the rest of my life until my next visit with Ishmael. I did not know then that I would see Ishmael much sooner than I had realized on my departure. Yet he is continually in my heart.

IX

Meditation and Meeting

I NEED YOU, MY trusted friend and teacher, Eliezer. I have learned much in reuniting with Ishmael that I would like to discuss with you. I hope that when I see you again, you will have news of finding me a wife. Now I will dismount from the donkey. I need to sort through the rush of thoughts that swirl through my mind like floods in the desert. I will sit under this broom tree.

Eliezer, I remember that you told me how you followed Abraham's call to El Shaddai. Ishmael taught me about his God, Chai Ro'i, the living, protecting God. Chai is the only and exclusive God for Ishmael. Ishmael's experience of the divine is undivided, unitary, as is Abraham's. The God Ishmael encountered embodies, not demands, but the fullness of compassion. Since Moriah, I cannot accept El Shaddai. I cannot praise his ways or be open to his oppressive demands. They are blood-curdling and spirit-crushing.

I have learned from Ishmael and from Melchizedek that my God does not tell me to be a vassal in an unequal Covenant. My God is the model for strength and humility.

My God encourages me to judge my actions and to restrain my impulses. With my God, there is clarity of vision and a sense of wholeness. The channels to my God are connecting with other people with respect and kindness, seeking reconciliation and peace.

I call my God Pachad Yitzach—the One I Hold in Awe—and also Gevurah—Source of Might. For I have learned I can be fully in relationship only through the awe I feel in the presence of another person. I need to draw upon the might of Gevurah to be open, supportive, and giving. These qualities, rooted in my God, enabled me to reach out to my brother, Ishmael.

The broom tree under which I sit stands firm in the face of hot east winds. With my God, I stand firm in the presence of enemies and friends. I know in my heart, Eliezer, that you will understand me and encourage my path.

I feel light. I am a desert vulture soaring on currents of dry, warm air. Freedom and renewed brotherhood are my wings.

Be'er Sheva is a place of plodding. It weighs me down and pulls me toward the cracked and arid land. Ishmael welcomes my presence at Be'er Lachai Ro'i. Here I fly with unbounded joy. I am more a native of this place than anywhere else in Canaan. In Be'er Sheva, I was in exile from my brother, from my true God, from the fullness of myself and of the future. I am at my place now, near Ishmael. I am home. I am rooted by the side of Chai's oasis of clear waters and sustaining love. After I return to Be'er Sheva to meet the bride you are bringing me, Eliezer, she and I will return to this place of orchards and shade. I am confident that Father will neither need nor miss us since he has his new wife, Keturah. I have no doubt about my path. I will walk it in confidence with Gevurah.

A gentle breeze curls around this broom tree. It carries the aroma of acacia and ziziphus. The early spring annuals of white, yellow, and deep red poke out of their rocky homes. They burst out joyously, like my blossoming spirit. The living sounds of the desert plants in the wind seem to be playing a song. I hear a tinkling of bells or of chimes pushed by the wind. This desert awakens all my senses. In the midst of my quiet absorption, I am alive to the life surrounding me.

The bells on the breeze get louder, and in a few moments, they grow more emphatic. I look to the east. On the horizon, a caravan of ten camels seems to be approaching. I wonder whether Ishmael has traded with them or raided them. I suspect the caravan has bypassed Ishmael, as it looks full of merchandise and is moving at a calm pace. It is coming toward me. I will conclude my meditations with a headstand to clear my thoughts and concentrate my mind.

. . .

"Eliezer." Rebekah breaks into his musings. "Look at that man standing on his head next to the broom tree. Except for that donkey, he is by himself in this desert."

"Indeed, he is an unusual sight. I only know of one person who used to stand on his head regularly. Wait until we get closer to him. Perhaps, either on his head or back on his feet, he will speak with us."

Eliezer, Rebekah, and the caravan continue treading the gravel path. After a short while, Eliezer speaks to Rebekah. "Rebekah, it seems that you will not have to wait until we get to Be'er Sheva to meet Isaac. My master's son is over there, feet in the air and head hovering above the cracked soil. I suspect it is Isaac because of his firm stance and intense concentration. We will interrupt him to introduce him to his wife."

"This serious, solitary man, whose name means 'He Laughs,' is to be my husband? I will veil my face as is proper, but really, I am not so proper. This stolid man looks like he needs a laugh. As is his name, so let him be. Watch me help him laugh."

Rebekah puts on her veil. She pulls herself out of her camel's saddle and moves forward beyond the camel's hump to its neck. She gets up carefully to balance on the camel's neck. She stands up and begins to wave her arms in Isaac's direction. As he looks up at her and stands on his feet, Rebekah bends over, holding the camel's neck, and stands on her hands. In about three breaths, she flings herself over her camel's head and lands on her feet, facing Isaac. Then she again wraps her face in the translucent veil.

Isaac is astonished. His brows go up, and his mouth gives up roars of laughter as he bends over, holding his stomach.

Never has he seen a grown woman toss herself and do tricks like an eight-year-old girl. How would her father allow her to behave in such a way? Isaac catches his breath. He walks toward the woman. He looks at the man who attends her. It could not possibly be her father. No—who, what? It is his confidant and mentor, Eliezer.

"Eliezer, my dear friend, I did not expect to meet you again until I got to Be'er Sheva."

"Consider our meeting fortuitous—certainly a blessing. I would have already been back to Be'er Sheva if this young woman's family had not slightly delayed our departure from Haran."

"From Haran? This bold and agile woman must be the wife you are bringing me. She is certainly fair of form. I have no doubt that her veil conceals a beautiful face. I do ask you, Eliezer, not to tell Abraham about her lively way of greeting me, which brings laughter back to me."

"You may be sure I will not share this with my master, Abraham. Now, greet your wife-to-be, Rebekah. She is the daughter of Bethuel, son of Nahor, brother of Abraham. I have found for you a precious cousin whose kindness overflows like a freshly dug well of water."

"Rebekah, I have waited a long, long time for this moment of meeting. You are precious to me even now. Let us go together to Be'er Sheva to meet the rest of our family and to celebrate our marriage."

"As you say, Isaac. Let us go to your family's camp. Our marriage frees me from the pain of Haran and fills me with hope for our partnership."

"Let's walk, Rebekah. No doubt you need to stretch after long hours in the saddle, despite your recent trick on the camel."

"That's just what I need, Isaac. It seems that you exercise your body and refresh your spirit in the outdoors. Nature has nurtured and restored me throughout my life and beyond my suffering. Before we walk, I want to let my maid, Deborah, know. She has looked after me since childhood and serves me even now. She is more of a mother to me than my own mother. Deborah will readily understand my desire for private sharing with my husband-to-be."

"Do speak to Deborah. I'll wait for you here."

Isaac Unbound

Rebekah returns to Isaac. With her hand, she brushes Isaac's hand. Her breezy touch is to him like eating honey after days of hunger or being refreshed in the falling waters of Ein Gedi on a scorching day.

Isaac reaches to grasp her hand in his. Rebekah says, "Just a moment, Isaac. I need my hands to remove my veil. From this time on, I want us to see each other clearly, in the open, without deceit." Rebekah removes her veil deliberately, her eyes staring directly at Isaac's face. He stands without moving and returns her gaze. Then Isaac speaks words that seem to come from a deep, flowing well.

"'You are beautiful, my companion, my partner; your eyes are doves. Like a rose among thorns, so is my beloved among women!' Rebekah, these are words sung on wedding nights by Canaanite grooms to their brides. When I look at you, at your face, these words bubble up from my heart to my lips."

"Isaac, do your words mean that tonight is to be our wedding night? I had imagined you would have wanted to wait until we arrive at Be'er Sheva to the tents of Abraham and Sarah."

"Indeed, I would like to become one with you, like waters flowing together from springs into a well. But, instead of setting up our tent at the well of Sheva, I would prefer to unite near the well of Chai Ro'i, which is not far from here."

Rebekah answers, "As that is your heart's desire, so it is my desire to be at that place for our union."

"We will need most of the day tomorrow to arrive at Be'er Lachai Ro'i. Then tomorrow will be our wedding night in our tent by the oasis."

"Isaac, what does Be'er Lachai Ro'i mean to you?"

As Isaac and Rebekah continue their walk in the desert, he tells her of his brother, her cousin, Ishmael. He relates how he adored Ishmael from his toddler days, how Ishmael and his mother, Hagar, were exiled with such cruelty. Isaac shares how, after Sarah died, he decided to go to Paran to find Ishmael in hopes of restoring and renewing their brotherly bonds. Rebekah learns from Isaac that little by little, through sincere outreach, love, and empathy, Ishmael accepted Isaac's summons to brotherhood.

Meditation and Meeting

"Until your arrival this day, Rebekah, the months I spent with Ishmael at Be'er Lachai Ro'i were the most peaceful and satisfying I have known in my life. I grew more confident and directed as a result of my stay with my brother. He developed the ability to look inward and be more accepting. We loved being in each other's presence."

"Then, I too will love being with Ishmael and his family at the oasis of Be'er Lachai Ro'i," replies Rebekah.

X

Comfort

As a pink dawn rises above the mountains of Moab to the east, the camp of Isaac and Rebekah is packing up tents and rugs for the day's trek to Be'er Lachai Ro'i. Rebekah has slept in her tent with Deborah. Isaac has joined Eliezer in his tent of speckled sheep skins. Rebekah and Isaac had each told their tent partners what it was like for them to meet their intended spouse. One could imagine a scribe writing a scroll from which Isaac and Rebekah spoke nearly identical sentiments. Rebekah describes to Deborah that she feels an inner strength in Isaac, a sustaining strength that would always guide their lives. Isaac describes to Eliezer his feeling that Rebekah is the mosaic piece that has been missing in his life: openness, gentleness, and integrity. Eliezer indicates his agreement since he has gotten to know Rebekah on the long journey from Haran. Isaac continues his description, saying she reminds him of an apple of Ein Gedi—fair of form, ready to burst with seeds of fertility. Deborah and Eliezer see the divine hand in this match of cousins—a union of strength, mutual support, and comfort.

Ishmael has been told by his sons that a caravan is approaching. Since he does not know the identity and origin of this troop, he comes out with an armed troop of his own. As the two groups draw near to one another, Isaac calls to Ishmael.

"Brother, come meet my bride, your soon-to-be sister-in-law, Rebekah!"

"What brings you back so soon, Isaac? Weren't you to return to Be'er Sheva?"

"Chai Ro'i created a surprise for me. Yesterday, I met Eliezer, who was returning from Haran with the woman I am to marry. I decided I would rather celebrate our marriage with you here and not hurry back to Be'er Sheva."

"Your return and your wedding in our midst bless our dwellings and this oasis. Welcome! Rest yourselves. We will prepare your wedding feast."

"Thank you, brother. With your kind permission, I would like to show Rebekah the oasis and your fields. I also wish to tell her of Chai Ro'i and how this God has blessed your life."

"Go, Isaac. I shall send for you and Rebekah when the feast is ready."

Isaac and Rebekah begin their stroll around the oasis. Isaac takes her to see the golden fields of barley and wheat. They stand in silence, holding hands, enveloped in the afternoon light.

"Rebekah, yesterday in our first conversation during our walk, you mentioned your pain and suffering in Haran. Would you tell me about this? Perhaps I can help you bear it and take you beyond it."

"It is a difficult matter to share with you. During my days of travel from Haran, I have thought about when to tell you. What has been my humiliation Deborah knows, but she is sworn to silence. Isaac, even in one day, I have seen in you signs of strength and understanding. I feel I can share with you safely. I believe I must tell you what you may realize in any case.

"I will always be at your side to comfort and protect you, Rebekah. My ears and my heart are listening."

"Isaac, I am not a virgin. Since I was eleven years old and for the past four years, my brother, Laban, would come into my tent and thrust himself into me. Indeed, his intrusion many nights a week was a sword piercing my inner parts. I could not stop him. I could not complain to my mother, who would not dare stand up to the men in our family. My father, Bethuel, was always passive and abhorred any confrontation. Deborah, my maid, was aware of Laban's use of me, but she is a slave whom Laban would have murdered if she spoke out. Deborah did hold me to comfort me. She also got sponges and showed me how to insert them to avoid pregnancy. She has been my only support until now."

Tears are pooling in Isaac's eyes and overflowing down his cheeks. "My dear Rebekah, my precious bride, I do not see you as deflowered. You were not with your brother, Laban, by choice or out of lust. You were constrained and forced. To me, you remain a virgin. You are pure in your love and devotion. More I cannot ask. I cannot imagine the depth and duration of your pain and suffering. I will be here, sharing our tent and being one another's comfort."

"Thank you, my dear husband. Not a man in ten thousand would be so loving and supportive. I never thought I could share my pain until this moment of being with you."

The shadows in twilight grow long. Isaac and Rebekah walk back to the camp in silence. There is no need to speak; just being with each other fills the space. Hands touching, fingers twined, point toward a complete physical union after the feast ends. As they draw near the tents of Ishmael, flutes begin to trill, and clay drums covered with stretched goat skins set a rhythm of celebration. Isaac and Rebekah join the circle of family and lifelong servants. Bowls of yogurt with cucumbers, leeks, and bread steaming from clay ovens are placed before the bride and groom. Wine pressed from the grapes of Ishmael's vineyards as well as Egyptian beer purchased from traders stand in jugs within easy reach of every person. Rebekah and Isaac make sure to limit their drinking to avoid being overcome by sleep. When the trays of roasted lamb on beds of toasted wheat, almonds, and raisins are served, they realize how ravenous they are. Midway through the feast, Ishmael stands up and signals for silence. All around the circle, talking stops and morsels are swallowed.

"My dear family, years ago, when I nearly perished from thirst and desert heat in a place not far from here, Chai Ro'i took compassion on my mother, Hagar, and me. Chai opened Mother's awareness to this very spring of water, which flows here and continues to sustain us. As Chai Ro'i promised, I have become the father of twelve sons, who someday will present me with grandchildren. We will grow from being a clan into many strong nations. We are blessed by Chai Ro'i. Now it is Isaac's turn to receive Gevurah's long-reserved blessing. Rebekah is his first blessing, and Isaac is hers. May Gevurah make you and Rebekah the parents of a great nation, a model of strength and wisdom for all peoples. So I bid you to go to your tent. Do your part to fulfill Gevurah's plan for your flourishing future."

Everyone around the circle nudges each other and laughs. Isaac especially laughs with unbound happiness.

Then, Ishmael takes up his own drum and sings the love song of Canaan. "You are beautiful, my partner, my bride; your eyes are doves."

Isaac and Rebekah get up from their places of honor in the circle. They walk to their tent to the ululations of the woman and the cheers of the men filling their ears.

As they enter the tent, Isaac says, "My beautiful bride, I need to tell you I am breathless with excitement but also quite nervous. I have never been intimate with a woman."

"Isaac, don't worry. We will learn together how to pleasure and fulfill each other. I promise you I will never be disappointed. I will never hesitate to tell you what I need. I expect you to be direct and open with me so that I may always be your loving wife. Now, before we lie down together, there is one sacred task I must perform."

Rebekah goes to a large goat skin sack in the corner of the tent. She has brought it on her journey from her home in Haran. She unties the mouth of the sack and withdraws from it a sizable clay jug. Isaac notices that a moon and stars and camels and shepherds are painted on it. Rebekah takes the jug and goes outside the tent to the waters of the oasis, which are a few steps away. She fills the jug and comes back to the tent. She places it outside the tent flap, where beams from the full moon will shine into it all through the night.

Isaac Unbound

When Rebekah enters the tent, Isaac asks her what has become of the jug she had taken out of the pack.

"I filled it with the water of Chai's oasis. I left the jug of water outside to catch the blessing of moonbeams through the night. The beams impart divine blessings to the water. In the morning, I will sprinkle our tent with that water, praying that our tent will always be an abode of peace and wholeness."

"Rebekah, I am in awe; I am speechless. My mother, Sarah, used to capture moon-blessed water in her jug to sprinkle on our tents. Our tents were always blessed except once, but that is a story for another day."

"Did you not know, Isaac, that all the women of Terach's family had such water jugs and served as priestesses of the moon god?"

"My father, Abraham, never prevented Sarah from sprinkling the blessed water over and around our tents. He did not allow her, though, to speak of a moon god or of any god except his own El Shaddai."

"Isaac, if your kindness and strength are inspired by your God, Gevurah, then Gevurah will be my only God. By his ways we will live, and we will teach those ways to our children. Now come onto this rug and lie with me. We need to make that first child."

Isaac brushes light kisses over Rebekah's face and neck. He caresses her breasts. She gently touches his covenanted member. He explodes and squirts mightily. Such is the result of a lifetime of celibacy and years of self-restraint. But after long years, he has much seed to sow. After a brief rest, Rebekah and Isaac unite in ecstasy four times. Rebekah whispers to Isaac, "Clearly, Gevurah has given you the gift of might. Your every touch is perfect, as though you committed to memory the map of my body."

Isaac smiles and thinks to himself how Eliezer has mentored him yet again. That afternoon, before the marriage feast, Eliezer had pulled Isaac aside.

Eliezer had said to Isaac, "If you will let me share a few words about your union with Rebekah, I suggest you approach her gently. Go on the path at her speed, not at your speed. Be patient with her and with yourself. Listen with your ears, your fingers, and your heart, and you will please her and lift both of you to the clouds."

Despite the totality of their union in body, mind, and spirit and even with an abundance of growing love, Rebekah does not conceive on the wedding night. She will remain barren for years to come.

In the early morning light, Rebekah removes herself from Isaac's arms. She arises from their sheep skins. She slips into her dress, which is embroidered with the moon in its different phases. She leaves the tent carrying a spoon made of a small gourd. She dips the spoon into the jug and takes up its waters, which have been blessed by lunar light. Holding the spoon of water, Rebekah stands still. She closes her eyes briefly, opens them, and offers a prayer.

"May Gevurah, whom Ishmael calls Chai, bless our tents and our encampment with calm, understanding, and openness." Rebekah sprinkles water with the spoon toward the tent flap. "May Gevurah guard us from blindness and open our eyes to the truth." Rebekah sprinkles another spoonful of water toward the tent. "May Gevurah keep far from our tents deceit and falsehood, jealousy, and strife." More water is dashed around the tent's perimeter. "May Gevurah bless us with the spirit of forgiveness and with the power of reconciliation and love." Rebekah dips again into the jug and this time fills the palm of the spoon to its brim. She tosses the water into the air. The droplets seem to be suspended in the space above the tent doorway.

Isaac has been listening to Rebekah's prayer, and to the water sprinkling. Outside the tent, he sees Rebekah drying and wrapping the spoon in a linen cloth. She lifts up the jug of water to pour its contents onto the desert floor. The water floods the patchwork of cracked earth, which has been like a brown and gray mosaic. As the water flows over the ground, it turns the cracks into a muddy pool, uniting everything within its reach.

Isaac lifts his gaze from the quenched ground and looks above the tents. He sees a small, pure white cloud hovering in the air over the tent. Isaac thinks some people would be amazed to see such a cloud. Others would disbelieve what they see. Isaac recalls that a cloud used to appear over Sarah's tent for many years, and light from it would illumine her dwelling. Isaac now approaches Rebekah. He hugs her to him for a long while. He is at last comforted, for he senses his mother's presence.

XI

Returning

REBEKAH AND ISAAC REMAIN with Ishmael and his family for twenty years. It is like being shaken out of a beautiful dream when Eliezer appears again at Be'er Lachai Ro'i. After Isaac brings water to wash the dust from Eliezer's feet and while a welcome meal is being prepared, Isaac silently awaits for Eliezer to tell the reason for his journey from Be'er Sheva.

"Isaac, I come here after leaving you with your brother nearly twenty years ago. I return now at Abraham's bidding. He asks you to come to him at Be'er Sheva. He wishes to meet his great-niece, Rebekah, and grandchildren born at this oasis. My master is growing old. El Shaddai has not addressed him since Moriah. He needs your filial presence."

"I understand, Eliezer. We will go to him. We have stayed here these many years not to avoid seeing Abraham. I do think my time with Melchizedek in Yevus helped purge me of my rage against my father. What kept us here was the restful water at this oasis with its green pastures and the growth of our flocks. My brother, Ishmael, has been a loving host from whom I did not wish to separate. But you are right. Abraham needs us, and we may need him as well."

Isaac tells Ishmael the reason for Eliezer's visit and that he has decided to accede to Abraham's request. Ishmael is saddened by the news. Tears flow down his cheeks, softening his wild ass reputation.

Isaac Unbound

"I cannot accompany you, Isaac, as you deserve and as I have already explained. Let me know when Father passes, and I will meet you at the burial cave of Machpelah by Mamre near Kiryat Arba. May Chai Ro'i, or rather Gevurah, protect you."

Two days later, Isaac and Rebekah finish packing and loading their tents, possessions, and provisions. Eliezer and his servants herd Isaac's flock of sheep and goats, which form the core of his growing wealth.

On the way north from Paran, as the donkeys, camels, and flocks plod their way, Rebekah begins a conversation that Isaac had avoided for twenty years of their marriage.

"Since we are going to the tents of Abraham and Keturah, Isaac, I need to understand your resistance to seeing him before now. Do not be reluctant to tell me because you know my heart's passion and compassion for you is an unquenchable flame."

"My hesitation to see Father as well as withholding his beautiful daughter-in-law from meeting him is complicated, not so much a matter of reason but certainly of stormy emotion. When I was a boy of thirteen years old, Abraham woke me one morning before dawn. He told me we would journey to a mountain in the land of Moriah to offer a sacrifice to El Shaddai. I was excited beyond measure to be going alone with Father on such a sacred journey. We saddled and loaded the donkeys and set off with two servant boys. I didn't consciously notice at first, but at the beginning of our journey, some things seemed odd to me. If we were intending to make a sacrifice to El Shaddai, why did Father fail to bring a kid from the sheep or goats? He did remember to bring a flint stone and a slaughtering knife. One of the donkeys bore a bound bundle of sticks and boughs. Why carry wood such a distance when there was probably abundant forest closer to the destination? I got up the courage to ask Father about the absence of a lamb. He said, 'Don't worry. El Shaddai will provide the lamb for the burnt offering.' His answer left me puzzled because I understood that only a domestic animal from one's own herd was a valid offering. A captured wild beast that costs the hunter nothing personally is not a true sacrifice.

"As we approached the top of the appointed place of sacrifice, Abraham unbound the bundle of wood. He told me to hold out both my arms and loaded me with the wood. Then he told the servants to stay in the place where we stopped. He told them we would sacrifice and then return to them. Those words bolstered my certainty that together we would make an offering to El Shaddai. The two of us walked on together until we reached the peak of Moriah. We sat and rested for a few minutes. Abraham told me to gather rocks to build an altar. He also commanded me to lay out the wood we brought on the altar. I did as I was bidden.

"Father was sitting on a boulder. He motioned for me to stand in front of him. As I stood facing him, he took a rope and began to wind it around my arms. As he bound me, he said, 'El Shaddai came to me a few days ago. My God commanded me to bring you here to offer you up as a burnt offering.'

"'Father,' I said in choking terror, 'that is what the other people of Canaan do, not the followers of El Shaddai!'

"'Isaac, today we will find out for a certainty if El Shaddai is similar to the gods of Canaan. I am staking your life and my future on the fact that, in the end, El Shaddai will provide an actual lamb for the sacrifice. So sure am I of this outcome that I said to the servants that we, both of us, would return to them. Nevertheless, we must follow through with each step of the commanded sacrifice.'

"Father lifted my bound body and placed me face up on the wood of the altar. Beyond the pain of the wood gouging my back and even beyond the fear of the slaughtering knife that would likely plunge into my chest or slit my throat, I felt utterly shattered and broken. My father had deceived me and failed to reject El Shaddai's cruel command. He did not attempt to protect me. My trust was now in shards, even as the blue sky I saw through the branches above me looked fragmented and broken. I was shivering with cold fright. Father's tears were running down his cheeks and splashing on my cheeks. He raised the knife, then hesitated for what seemed like an unending interlude. He dropped the knife, looked up, and ran in the direction of a bleating ram caught in the thicket. I wriggled out of my bonds and got off the altar. I ran in the opposite direction of where Father went. I ran to the town of Yevus, just down from Moriah. It turned out that in the palace of its king, Melchizedek, I was saved and safe. I stayed with Melchizedek. I remained for a year. He guided me through a healing practice six days a week."

Rebekah listens intently to Isaac's recounting of his horrendous experience. She did not want to interrupt him with questions until this moment.

"Isaac, who could possibly know the angst and terror you felt, especially in the face of Abraham's shredding your life and smashing your trust? Can you explain to me how Melchizedek healed you?"

"Melchizedek had a variety of ways of helping, if not totally curing me. These ways included immersing myself in the purest water and basking in the various colors of glass globes and vases. He helped me understand that El Shaddai wanted Abraham to model a faith that does not require the sacrifice of human beings. He suggested that the expression of the strength of Abraham's trust and reliance on El Shaddai was that he took me up Mount Moriah at El Shaddai's command. He helped me understand that Abraham's love for me was so deep and fierce that Abraham never would have gone through all the preparations and journey for my sacrifice if he had thought El Shaddai would have him murder me. Abraham revealed his trust in El Shaddai when he told the servant lads, to whom he had no need to explain anything, that we would return. Only at the time I was in Melchizedek's care did I see those words to the servants as a mere deception to lull me into cooperation. It took sometime before I grasped that Father believed his own words. When I understood that, I told Melchizedek I could forgive and reconcile with Father."

"My precious husband, your experience with Abraham is chilling. It is hardly conceivable that a father would behave with guile to blindly follow such a command from his god."

"More than that, Father did not allow me to bid farewell to my mother, Sarah, before we left for Moriah. I had never been far from her, and the departure without a goodbye was like an initial binding foretelling, unbeknownst to me, what would come. I have also concluded that Mother had no idea of Father's plan. I learned from Eliezer that Mother died within days of Father's return from Moriah. When Father did not come back to her at Kiryat Arba, she assumed that I was dead. This was more than she could bear. Her spirit withered, and she died. So said Eliezer."

"Isaac, I am beginning to understand why, after all these years, you did not plan to return to Abraham's camp and why you did not share your frightful story with me."

"Tell me what you think, Rebekah. I continue in my heart to resist this return. To be truthful, it is almost too much to contemplate as each step of the donkeys brings us toward Be'er Sheva."

"Isaac, you said that after your time with Melchizedek, after the increased understanding he gave you, you were ready to forgive Abraham and to reconcile with him. Yet you have not stood in his presence and done so. Is it possible you have not been ready for such a meeting? Are you fully prepared to face the pain and anger the thought of him stirs inside you?"

"Rebekah, it is clear that you not only listen intensely to words, but you also hear the murmurings of the heart."

"This is what my innermost hearing tells me, Isaac. You need to confront your father. You need to let him know of your rage and hurt over his keeping you from Sarah and how his actions may have hastened her death. You can disavow his guile and deception as a means to act in the name of El Shaddai. I think it would also be well for you to tell Abraham of your personal relationship with Gevurah and of your rejection of the nature and character of El Shaddai."

"Rebekah, you are so full of wisdom and insight. You bless my life. What you suggest I do, I know, is necessary. It feels overwhelming, even too much, to place my feelings before Father. He carries himself with such dignity, almost like royalty. He is barely approachable."

"Just be assured, Isaac, that I know well your feelings and your determination to keep your memories locked away. For the same reasons, I did not hesitate to go with Eliezer to become your wife. My father, Bethuel, let me down again and again by pretending not to know that Laban sneaked into my tent to force himself on me. Eliezer was my means of escape. The money and gifts he offered Laban were more alluring to my brother than my body. I took the only chance I saw to free myself. You have turned out to be my soulmate and my life's blessing."

"And you are mine as well. We have several days until we arrive at Be'er Sheva. I am preparing myself to present Abraham with the truth of what is in my mind and heart. From that point on, responsibility for his relationship with me will be his. To these ends, I pray for that Gevurah will strengthen me."

XII

Contraction

KADESH IS AN OASIS at the southern boundary of Canaan. Rebekah and Isaac set up camp there to rest before a long day's trek to Be'er Sheva. The lush waters of Kadesh make it a meeting place for a palette of clans and tribes—Hittites, Canaanites, Amalekites, and Philistines. None of these groups claims ownership of Kadesh. They share its water and fruit, trade news and journey stories, and greet each other without formalities. Except for the Philistines, all of them speak the same language with a few differences in pronunciation and specific vocabulary. These shades of language enrich the speech of each group. Only the Philistines keep to themselves. They have, over time, included enough Canaanite words in their speech for trade, but they continue to speak the tongue they brought from across the Great Sea.

While Isaac and Rebekah relax outside their tent in the cool of a desert twilight, a Philistine approaches them. He speaks a broken Canaanite.

"Name me, Phicol."

"I am Isaac. This is my wife, Rebekah."

"Beautiful, very beautiful. King mine want to know beautiful woman. Come to Azzah to meet her to king."

"Don't you know that we Canaanites do not show off our women? We cannot come to Azzah, and we will never go to the territory of the Philistines."

"Ah, bad to say to me. Like throwing dirt in well of mine."

"I am sorry, Phicol. I am not one who throws dirt in wells. I dig them out and clean them. Excuse us now. Rebekah and I walk at this twilight time every day."

As Phicol leaves, stomping with insult, Isaac and Rebekah walk east with the setting sun warming their backs.

"What a strange man was that Philistine," Rebekah says.

"I have an odd sense that I have met him in the past. The Philistines think they are superior to us Canaanites—more civilized and advanced. That point in his self-understanding frees him of restraint and allows him unlimited brazenness. That is exactly the reason I will avoid setting foot in the land of the Philistines, now or ever."

They walk a distance from Kadesh, where they can barely hear the voices of people at the oasis. A few paces to their right, they see a square of ground bordered by rocks, each the size of a fist. At the top of the square is a vertical slab of granite rock made of pink quartz and black flecks of obsidian. In the center of the slab, carved into it, is a female figure with her arms raised and a crescent moon above her.

"What is this place, Isaac? It looks like a shrine."

"You are right, Rebekah. It is a sanctuary without an altar. As I look at the female figure on the slab, it is similar to representations of the Egyptian goddess Isis. This is probably a shrine to Isis erected by Egyptian desert guards or by Egyptian miners of copper."

"This place vibrates for me, Isaac. I feel here that heaven takes note of me, cares for me. It is like being in a throbbing womb whose power ripples my own womb. Somehow, I feel this place signals the end of my barrenness. The spirits of children are calling to me."

"Rebekah, I know how our lack of children saddens you and crushes you under a weight of despair. Does what you are feeling in this place foretell your swelling with a child?"

"Isaac, I have never asked you before, but would you here, in this place, set a plea before Gevurah to open my womb, to create the family we are promised?"

At first, for just a flicker of a moment, Isaac demurs in his heart. How can he make a plea to Gevurah in a foreigner's sanctuary to a female image? He is quickly in touch with that which makes his faith unique. He remembers that while Gevurah means the Mighty One, Gevurah is a feminine word in its structure. Gevurah contains both the masculine and the feminine. He also reflects that nothing requires greater might than bearing a child. And this is a foreign shrine? How can any place be foreign where humans seek a connection to the divine?

"Rebekah, I have been remiss by not giving voice to your longing—to our yearning—for a child. I will place our plea, our hope, before Gevurah. Let us enter this square together."

Isaac takes Rebekah's hand. They step over the stone boundary. They are silent. Rebekah places her hands on Isaac's hips. He places his hands, together yet open like the wings of a dove, on Rebekah's womb. Isaac prays:

> "Gevurah, Source of Strength and Awe
> Your infinite might sustains life
> All life is your gift of unity to the living;
> Extend your life giving might to Rebekah.
> Open her forlorn womb.
> Make it like a fruitful field
> Whose harvest will be sons and daughters.
> Establish and make firm our reliance upon you.
> There is no God like you, Mighty One.
> You bring us into life and cause us to flourish.
> Grant Rebekah and me your mighty force of life."

After the words of this prayer, which Isaac offers spontaneously, Rebekah hugs him.

"I know, Isaac, that Gevurah has heard your prayer and will respond when the season is ready. Thank you, my dear husband."

"Rebekah, I prayed for myself as much as for you. Are we not to fulfill our Covenant with Gevurah through producing children, nurturing them, and teaching them?"

"Yes, Isaac, but I think Gevurah does not expect us to rely entirely on divine might. Let's go back right away to our tent. Plant your seed in the soil of my renewed womb. This time I have confidence that Gevurah will add the water of life, and soon the harvest will be full."

"Rebekah, I appreciate your religious fervor. I am more than ready to do the gardening."

Isaac and Rebekah make tender love, yet with ardor. They are committed to their sacred task. Rebekah whispers to Isaac that she wishes all commandments were as pleasurable to fulfill. Isaac laughs and agrees. The two fall asleep, but Isaac is restless and his sleep fitful. A strange dream invades his mind. He turns from side to side, then yells, "Dig men, dig!" Rebekah wakes and shakes Isaac awake.

"Isaac, you were thrashing and shouting in your sleep!"

"I was having an odd dream. It is still vivid to me. We are in the land of the Philistines to escape some sort of drought or famine in Canaan. I see myself. I know it is I. I feel so because you are by my side. Yet, when I see myself, my face is the face of Abraham. A Philistine with spear and shield approaches. He speaks gruffly in fluent Canaanite. I know he is the same Phicol we met yesterday afternoon. He speaks to me: 'Don't tell me this beautiful woman with you is your sister. We know she's your wife. We see your playful behavior, the foreplay you think is private behind the tent curtain. My king, Abimelech, wants nothing to do with you. He has ordered me to fill in the wells you recently dug and to tell you to leave his kingdom.'

"I say, 'We mean no harm or threat to Abimelech. We merely want to farm, and we will share our produce with the king.'

"'You must leave now,' Phicol answers.

"We pack our camp and move southeast into the vicinity where Abraham had told me he had settled for a time. In my dream, I discover the wells my father's servants had dug many years before. I tell my own servants to dig the dirt and rubble out of Abraham's wells. They work furiously until water comes up, clear and clean. We wet the cracked ground until it is smooth. We use clay jugs that look identical to Sarah's and your jars. The water sinks in, and we plow furrows and sow seeds. Like a miracle, wheat, barley, and grapes spring up. We have planted only a small section of ground, enough for our own food supply. Now these crops cover ground a hundred times greater than our planting. The mighty Gevurah has done His work.

"We harvest a bit of our crops and sit here for a meal of celebration. As we are eating and talking, the Philistine king, Abimelech, and his retinue approach our camp.

"'Peace to you, Isaac, son of Abraham. I have met your parents in years past. It did not go well between us. Phicol told me he had met you at Kadesh. I come now to offer peace and hospitality in my kingdom.'

"In my dream, Rebekah, I remember thinking that this bloodsucking Philistine is attracted to our bounty. His hypocritical offer of hospitality is roused by his hopes of taxing large portions of our crop. Yet I decide it is better to make an ally, even a tepid one, than an enemy full of enmity. I answer Abimelech in a conciliatory tone.

"'Thank you, O King. We are blessed by your offer of peace and hospitality.'

"I invite Abimelech and his officers to sit and join our feast. This is perhaps beyond what the king has expected. My intention is that with the offer of our hospitality to him, he would be reasonable.

"As we are feasting, I ask the king what amount of rent he requires. He answers, 'I want to be fair. We will take 40 percent of your crops as rent. We will take another 40 percent as payment for the water you draw from under our land.'

"I reply, 'My men have dug out ancient wells. They have worked the land. My God makes everything thrive. You call taking 80 percent of our crops fair?'

"'In my country, I alone determine what is fair. Accept my generous offer or go to your parched Canaan.'

"'My God, Gevurah, will provide for us and for you as well. I accept your terms and your offer of peace.'

"A startled look comes over Abimelech. The ground begins to shake. It is an earthquake. Actually, Rebekah, it was you shaking me out of this dream."

"What do you think your dream means, Isaac?"

"It reinforces what I said to you and Phicol yesterday. I will never go to the land of the Philistines. I will place my trust only in Gevurah, who guides me to remain in Canaan for our entire lives. That is the only way to fulfill the promise that we will inherit Canaan."

...

As the dawn comes up, Isaac, Rebekah, and their servants are packed. They start out on what will be a full day to reach Be'er Sheva. Rebekah is on edge about meeting Isaac's father, whose reputation intimidates her.

"Isaac, tell me about Abraham. What is he like?"

"When my father came along, he broke the mold of what it meant to be a citizen of his home in Ur Kasdim. He broke with their idolatrous and immoral ways. When he saw that it was nearly impossible to live according to what his heart dictated, he resolved to leave. The force of his personality and the urgency of his vision were such that he convinced my grandfather, Terach, to come with him, along with his surviving brother, Nahor, and his deceased brother's son, Lot. He led the family north and west to Haran. My grandfather, Terach, could not continue the journey, so Abraham agreed to remain in Haran. When Terach died a few months after the family's arrival in Haran, my father gathered the family. He told them that El Shaddai had commanded him to go forth from his land, his birthplace, and his father's house. Now it was the right time to fulfill the rest of El Shaddai's charge—to go to a land El

Shaddai would signify. Nahor was not persuaded to leave Haran. This explains why your family did not join our family in Canaan."

"It sounds, Isaac, like your father is bold and strong, one with a pioneering urge and foresight. Few men can demonstrate such determination."

"It is true. Your impression of Abraham is valid. His strength is rooted in his reliance on El Shaddai. He believes El Shaddai sent him on his journey to meet a future of blessing for his clan and for all humanity.

"Big dreams. Swelling visions. Abraham decided to prove his loyalty to El Shaddai by circumcising himself and Ishmael. Abraham was elderly, and Ishmael was a young adult. At least, in my case, I was but eight days old when Abraham circumcised me. Already with that act, Abraham showed his willingness to impose his wishes on those under his tutelage and paternal authority.

"Abraham also has a honed sense of morality and justice. That sense gives him nearly unlimited courage to stand up to what he perceives as unjust. When El Shaddai revealed to him the divine plan to destroy the cities of Sodom and Gomorrah, Father strongly protested. He dared to confront El Shaddai, saying, 'What if there are fifty righteous people in the cities? Will you slay the righteous with the wicked, thus making them comparable. Will the Judge of all the earth not behave justly?'

"I have always held Father in the highest esteem, as a model of who I wish to be, for the way he stood up to El Shaddai against collective punishment and for fair treatment of the individual."

Rebekah raises an eyebrow.

"Isaac, your father did not stand up to El Shaddai when this god ordered your sacrifice. In the face of his pleading for Sodom and Gomorrah, was it not hypocrisy and cowardice that he did not stand up for your life? In the end, he sounds like one whose belief is beyond reason and outside the realm of the ethical. He appears to be drunk from imbibing El Shaddai's commands and too inebriated to exercise judgment."

"That is exactly the source of my distance from him. Despite the strong possibility that he intuited that El Shaddai would spare me in the end on Moriah, he did not consider my feelings or Mother's. He did not take into his mind the damage his obedience to El Shaddai would cause Mother and me. He could not imagine that his compliance with El Shaddai would kill Mother and break my heart."

"Isaac, your father sounds like a man of contradictions, a difficult man to engage if one wishes to guard his own personality."

"You have clear insight, Rebekah. I also want to encourage you to rely on your own strength when you meet him. You can handle him, just as you told your father and brother you wished to leave them to marry me. You are strong. But, I also know that Abraham feels great nostalgia and love for your part of the family, even though they refused to leave Haran. He will doubtless feel that your presence at his camp as my wife completes the family's journey to Canaan, which El Shaddai promised to our descendants."

Isaac, Rebekah, and their group barely rest along the way. They reach Be'er Sheva and the camp of Abraham and Keturah just before sunset. Campfires send skyward orange sparks and leaping arms of flame. Abraham gets up from his place and limps over to Isaac. Father and son embrace for a time that seems frozen in amber. Both of them are weeping. Then Keturah breaks in.

"Abraham, greet Isaac's wife, Rebekah, your great-niece from Haran."

Abraham turns toward Rebekah. He freezes in amazement.

"Rebekah, my daughter, forgive me for staring. To me, you are the image of your great aunt Milcah; may her memory be a blessing. It is my deep honor and joy to welcome you to our family and to Be'er Sheva. But I must ask you, where are my grandchildren? Why do you hide them from their grandfather?"

"Father Abraham, I am sorry to tell you my womb has been closed up for many years. I have been barren. A few days ago, Isaac offered a plea to Gevurah to open my womb. Somehow, in the depth of my heart and the core of my womb, I feel I will bear children in the near future."

CONTRACTION

"Yes, Father, our faith in Gevurah is great. We know with a certainty that through Rebekah and me, El Shaddai's promise of descendants as numerous as the stars will come to pass."

"Rebekah, Isaac, I am very pleased to learn of your confidence that El Shaddai will bless your womb and your seed. Sarah and I had a similar experience and a long wait—not always with patience—for Isaac's birth. As a show of our faith, we need to continue to be patient. Now, my children, we will soon break bread and have a meal. Rebekah, let Keturah help you unpack and bathe. Isaac, come into my tent. Let's talk."

Isaac looks at Rebekah and gives her a half smile as though to say, "Here he goes with a summons and conversation on demand." Isaac follows his father into the tent.

"Sit, my son. Sit on the lush camel's-hair blankets. They are most comfortable."

Isaac sits, and the camel's-hair blanket seems to caress him. It is scented with jasmine and acacia, which bury the beastly odor of camel's fur. Whatever mud and dung the living camel may have immersed itself in is now forgotten. The perfume of living plants wafts from the camel blanket throughout Abraham's ample tent.

"Isaac, first I wish to ask you, how is my son Ishmael? How did you find him? You stayed with him a long time. It must have been pleasant."

"Father, Ishmael is well. He took me in and embraced me. He welcomed Rebekah. He is flourishing with flocks and herds and beautiful harvests. He has made you the grandfather of twelve boys. He is no longer the misbegotten wild ass of a man, but rather a prince among his fellows, a man respected for his wisdom and strength."

"As a father, his father, I am pleased to learn of Ishmael's character. How I long to see him, to seek his forgiveness."

"Candidly, Father, he will neither receive you nor call on you here. He and I spoke often and in depth of your exiling him and Hagar. He nearly perished in the Wilderness of Paran. His father is now Chai Ro'i, the God who saved him and Hagar by showing them a flowing spring. He still lives there, as you may know."

"What I did to him and to his beloved mother, Hagar, was an inexcusable act demanded by your mother and endorsed by El Shaddai. I wish I could make amends with them and earn their forgiveness."

"Father, some things are unforgivable. You must live with past decisions that impacted Ishmael and Hagar. If it is any slight comfort, Ishmael promised to join me at Machpelah when you lie next to Sarah in the grave. That will be his way of honoring you and supporting me. It will have to suffice."

Abraham exhales a long breath, a voiceless sigh.

"That past, Isaac, for me is present. I live with it and struggle daily with it."

"Father, do you also wrestle with taking me up to Moriah?"

"Yes, my son. I know it was hard on you, Isaac. I am sorry for your fright and the suffering that resulted. Nevertheless, I stand by El Shaddai's command to demonstrate to all Canaan that child sacrifice is ungodly and undesirable."

"Was there no other way to convey that lesson than to erase a son's trust in his father's protection? You shattered my relationship with you."

"Isaac, I do regret the effect your experience had on you. But I urge you to keep in mind that you were and continue to be the bearer of El Shaddai's Covenant within our family. It is incumbent upon us to be loyal to El Shaddai, follow his commands, and be fulfilled in His gifts and blessings to us."

"Father, I need you to know that my Covenant is not with El Shaddai. Did you not hear me speak of Gevurah outside the tent?"

"Who is Gevurah, Isaac? Did I not teach you of the real presence and power of El Shaddai, whose name means 'the God who is sufficient'? Did we not talk often of El Shaddai's promise to bless you as His Covenant partner?"

"Father, you experienced El Shaddai in Ur and Haran not only as the sole God of the universe, beyond time and space, but also as the master of human destiny. So you taught me from my earliest years. I accept and revere El Shaddai's call to walk before Him in righteousness. That charge to us is imperative if we are to banish evil and fashion justice in the world. But, Father, I also lived the ruthlessness of El Shaddai in your rigid adherence and blind following of your God. El Shaddai is not sufficient for me."

Abraham looks stricken and in pain. He appears shrunken in his corner of the tent. It is as though he has contracted inward and is occupying less space, both in his physical body and in his spirit. It is shocking because in my youth and his middle age, we looked so alike people would often confuse us and come to me for counsel thinking I was Abraham. This was not acceptable to Abraham's ego. He prayed to his God for some physical characteristics that would help people distinguish between us. El Shaddai complied and gave him wrinkles in his skin and lucent streaks of white in his hair and beard. Now, however, Abraham does not merely look elderly. He is in some way less imposing, more peaceful, and smaller in stature.

"Isaac, I did hear your reference to Gevurah. Tell me of this God you cling to."

"Gevurah is my God, whom I have experienced many times since our journey to Moriah. Gevurah's might has enabled me to be emotionally strong. Gevurah has encouraged me to carry on, to repair breaches in my relationships, and to be true to myself. Gevurah has led me to see the full humanity of others. I revel in my fellow humans' reflections of Gevurah even as I accept their follies and my own. I still accept El Shaddai's call to walk in righteousness. Yet, my experience of Gevurah encompasses El Shaddai's charge and calls on my total humanity. Gevurah is my Covenant partner."

"My son, I honor Gevurah and your Covenant with Gevurah. I hear clearly that your Covenant with Gevurah includes and continues mine with El Shaddai. You have learned what I set before you years ago. You have extended what you learned and expanded its moral vision. You have accepted the heritage I tried to convey and you have built upon it new understandings of your own. This is how it should be with father and son."

Isaac gets up from his place and goes over to Abraham. Father and son embrace. Isaac sees now that his contraction is not so much due to natural aging; it is a pulling back from the old positions of certainty, of axiomatic thinking, and of imposing his experience and understanding on those around him. He simply absorbs less space than he once did. Such personal contraction makes room for wholeness in the world.

XIII

Covenant Bearers

Toward the end of their third month in Be'er Sheva, Rebekah comes to Isaac with news of her pregnancy. They hug and cling to each other and weep tears of thanks.

"May Gevurah protect our seed and nurture it, Rebekah. May Gevurah guard your womb and its resident from all harm."

"May this be Gevurah's will, Isaac. Now, let us go with this news to Abraham."

As they approach Abraham's tent, with the door flaps open in each direction, they see Abraham sitting with Eliezer in deep discussion.

"Father, Eliezer, we wish to have a word with you."

"Isaac, Eliezer, and I are talking about our clan's future. My days are limited, and arrangements need to be made. Your presence is timely. I was about to send for you."

"I have news of the future—our clan's future—Father. Rebekah is pregnant! Her maid, Deborah, estimates she is nearly four full moons as an expectant mother."

"This is much-awaited news. I have longed for it, Isaac. I will see my grandchild before I die. He will bear the Covenant into the far times beyond us."

"Don't assume the child will be a male, Father. It could be a female who will grow in beauty and strength like Sarah. A daughter taught and guided in the ways of our family will become a woman who shapes the clan."

"You are right, Isaac. I will be blessed and will give thanks for a child born to you and Rebekah."

Three months have passed since Isaac told Abraham of his approaching time of becoming a grandfather. There is a lightness of expectation in the family. Frequent smiles and laughter fill the camp. Rebekah visits Abraham every day. The healthy visage she radiates shines on her great uncle. Abraham seems to be a mirror to her ebullient mood. On one visit, though, she is sad. Her face looks pinched and puzzled, and she is without her usual energy.

"My daughter, what is it with you? Have you forgotten today you will soon be a mother? What has happened to your joy?"

"Uncle, I have been in pain for several days now. My belly is constantly moving back and forth, with a lump here and a depression there. It hurts. It makes me wonder if the result is worth the agony. Other women bear a child without such struggle. Why me?"

"Rebekah, will you allow me to place my hand on your belly?"

"Yes, Uncle, but do you think you can learn more than my maid, Deborah? She has already whispered to me she thinks I am carrying twins."

"El Shaddai, your Gevurah, may help me to understand more."

"You have my permission; I am listening."

Abraham places his warm hand, with its translucent skin, on her dress over her womb. He closes his eyes and feels a burst of movement. He waits with his hand in place.

With a distant gaze, Abraham speaks: "Twins are in your womb. Two nations are within your body. Two peoples will come out of you. One people will be stronger than the other. The elder shall serve the younger."

Rebekah begins to cry. She thinks that after so many years of infertility, it is fair recompense that she carries two children. For this, she can praise Gevurah.

"Father Abraham, why must there be division between sons in my sons' generation? Isaac and Ishmael endured for years a separation not of their making. Now you foresee struggle and strife in my children's lifetime?"

"This, too, is a lesson from El Shaddai. There was from the beginning an inner circle and an outer circle, a favored one and one kept at a distance, a Covenant-bearer and one who is indifferent. It is the task of the Covenant-bearers to enlarge circles, to extend favor and grace, and to encompass each person in the Covenant of justice and love. From the time of our distant ancestor Cain and his brother, Abel, to Shem and Ham, and to Isaac and Ishmael, this is the challenge. Yours will be to encircle both your sons as one while recognizing their separateness."

"Thank you, Uncle. I will keep in mind what you have told me. I will try to shape Covenant-bearers."

When Rebekah reaches the end of her seventh month, Abraham dies. He had been failing, weakening, before their eyes. A gentle, accepting sadness flows in the camp. The sadness is not just for the loss of the father of the clan, but especially because he did not live a few more weeks to hold his twin grandsons. Isaac sends word to Ishmael to meet him in three days at the cave of Machpelah to bury Abraham.

Rebekah remains in Be'er Sheva.

XIV

The Interment of Abraham

ISAAC AND ISHMAEL INTER their father in his resting place next to Sarah in the cave of Machpelah. The brothers speak of the expansive personality of Abraham. They reminisce about how he showed himself to be a man of principle when he intervened to save his nephew, Lot, who was kidnapped during the battle of Canaanite kings. Once again, they tell the story of Abraham, who challenged El Shaddai's intention to destroy Sodom and Gomorrah. Ishmael recalls as well their father's unbending loyalty to El Shaddai.

Ishmael says, "He was rigid and unbending in his insistence that only El Shaddai is the true God who creates and acts in human affairs. He gathered all the force of his mind to carry out what he perceived was the will of El Shaddai."

Eliezer, who has been keeping a respectful silence, replies to Ishmael. "Your father grew in ways you could not know since, over the years, you neither visited his tents nor were present to him at Be'er Lachai Ro'i. Over the years, he continued to miss your presence. In his heart, he truly repented for exiling you and Hagar, but he could not complete his atonement by bringing you home. Sarah would have pounced on him like a leopard of the Aravah, tearing him to emotional shards. He never ceased loving you, his eldest son. He spoke of you frequently to me because he trusted my understanding and needed my support."

The Interment of Abraham

Ishmael stands in his place, voiceless, as tears stream down his cheeks. He chokes back sobs. He fears that if the dam of his emotions breaks, his cries will be heard throughout Canaan.

Eliezer continues, "There is something else, Ishmael, that you should know, and I think Isaac already has a sense of this. Abraham told me in his last month about the names of your Gods. He grasped, Isaac, that your Gevurah is the root of your personal strength to be a conciliator, to be one who tries to make the world whole. He said, Ishmael, that your only God, Chai Ro'i, preserves and guards your life and that of your clan at your oasis. He recognized that Chai Ro'i is the source of all life and being for you.

"Most notable is that on his death bed, Abraham whispered to me, 'Gevurah and Chai Ro'i are part of the reality of El Shaddai. What Isaac and Ishmael have done is enlarge the qualities of El Shaddai. None of us will know in entirety all of El Shaddai's nature. Through Isaac and Ishmael's individual experiences of what is whole, they have named their view of the Mighty One who enlivens the universe. At this late moment, I have learned from my sons. So it should be with all children—extending the teaching of the parents.'"

Isaac, Ishmael, and Eliezer bury Abraham in the floor of Machpelah. Isaac prays, "El Shaddai, watch over our father as he sleeps with his fathers. Gevurah, give us strength to bear and to share what Abraham taught us. Chai Ro'i, sustain us so we may never be in exile from one another."

The three men exit Machpelah and roll the boulder by the cave in front of its entrance. Ishmael and Isaac embrace. They promise to meet again. Isaac and Eliezer return to Be'er Sheva.

XV

Birth and Brit Milah

A FEW WEEKS LATER, after Isaac's return from burying Abraham, Rebekah endures a difficult labor. She bears twin sons, as had been foretold by Abraham. She and Isaac name them Esau and Jacob. They are not identical twins. Esau, who was born first, is of a ruddy complexion. He has a prolific shock of dark hair as well as a sort of hairy fuzz on his skin. He is far from being a beautiful infant. What surprises Rebekah when she first holds him are Esau's features. They are similar to those of the child's uncle, Laban. Esau's resemblance to her brother, Laban, arouses a churning in her stomach, a revulsion. She tells herself, "He is not Laban. He is an innocent child, my child. I am here for him."

As she nurses Esau, she feels his ravenous and ardent sucking. It is as though he wishes to have it all—her milk, her breast, her entire self, and perhaps even all their surroundings. She marvels, but with worry and fear, at how fiercely this little one pulls her breast toward himself and holds it so firmly.

When Esau finishes nursing and falls asleep, she takes up his brother, Jacob. He is smooth, without blemish or wrinkle. It is pleasant to gaze upon this serene face, which makes Rebekah feel calm and hopeful. He is the image of Isaac. He nurses slowly, not with difficulty but with a gradual pace that suggests confidence, a feeling of at-homeness. Who could imagine that this sweet-faced,

BIRTH AND BRIT MILAH

innocent child held his brother's heel at birth? It was as though Jacob could not wait to emerge to do his work in the world. Esau managed to prevail as though wildly determined to cling to the rights of the firstborn son. As she nurses her sons, she remembers Abraham telling their destiny. Will her firstborn, with all his strength, be surpassed by her gentle heel-grasper?

As the first week of the twins' lives goes by, Isaac becomes nervous and restless.

Isaac will have difficult work to do tomorrow. It will be the eighth day since the birth of Esau and Jacob. Isaac will remove their foreskins with a flint knife. He will bring them into the Covenant of Gevurah-El Shaddai, even as Abraham modeled decades ago. The ritual is called Brit Milah.

. . .

In the depth of the night, a trembling seizes Isaac in his sleeping covers. At first, it is mild. He thinks he has caught a chill. The more he wraps himself tightly in his robes and covers, the more intense becomes his shaking. He feels his stomach churning, a bile rising within his core. His trembling does not stop, even though he now feels like a searing copper smelter envelops him. He falls into a delirious sleep.

He yells, and his cries bring Eliezer from his own tent. Eliezer sees Isaac sweating, with glistening beads on his forehead like the dew on Mount Hermon.

"Isaac, wake up. Are you ill? You have been calling out in your sleep. You made noise like a bleating ram."

"It was horrible, Eliezer. I had a vision of myself standing over a stone altar with a flint knife in my hand. Father is standing behind me, forcing upward my hand holding the knife. On the altar are two little lambs staring at me, looking into my eyes, silent as the stone altar. I look up to the sky. Immediately, it cracks, with blue shards falling on me, on the lambs, and on the ground, but not on Father. I call to him, 'Where are the lambs for the offering?' He answers, 'Every generation will provide for itself lambs for the sacrifice.' Then Father gathers up the blue shards. He repairs the sky, but the cracks remain visible. You must have come in then, because this imagining ended abruptly."

"Isaac, have you an understanding or interpretation of your vision?"

"Now that I am awake and have recounted it, I do not think it requires magicians or shamans to explain it. For the last several months, I have dreaded the thought of performing Brit Milah on my sons. Tomorrow, that occasion will arrive. It is their eighth day since birth. It feels to me like what I experienced at Father's determined hand on Moriah. I am not sure I can or even want to perform the act."

"To be sure, it is no easy act to carry out, Isaac. No one feels ready to inflict pain by drawing blood from one's child. Yet you must do so. You know that."

"I am not sure I know that. How is this Milah truly a symbol of our Covenant with El Shaddai-Gevurah? Canaanites observe it. Egyptians observe it. People in Haran observe it. How is our practice different, and if it is not unique, how can it symbolize our Covenant?"

"Our Milah Covenant is not focused as much on the act itself as on its set time, the eighth day following birth."

Isaac acknowledges, "It is the case that I have heard of no other tribe or people who practice circumcision before age twelve. Father circumcised himself at age ninety-nine, and Ishmael at thirteen. Yet the command was carried out on me by Father on my own eighth day."

"Do you remember when Abraham brought you into the Covenant?"

"Of course not. I was an infant."

"That is the point, Isaac. Milah at eight days, while briefly painful for the infant, does not become a memory. The child recuperates quickly, as you are living evidence. Our Milah is a symbol of sensitivity, caring, and our commitment to teaching those qualities to our children through their growing up. Our goal is to create compassionate children who descend from compassionate parents."

"But the child has no say in the matter of Milah, any more than I did going up to the altar on Moriah."

"Isaac, there are many lessons and directions parents choose for children without asking them. We do so out of commitment to them, to shape their souls."

"Eliezer, I need to think deeply about your explanation, and it will take me time. But I did make a promise to Father to fulfill the ritual of Milah on the eighth day, on the morrow. I will do so with your help."

"What would you have me do, Isaac?"

"Rather than tie the boys down to restrain them, as happened to me at Moriah, would you hold the infants, one at a time, in your lap?"

"I accept your request, actually the honor, which you offer me."

"Thank you, Eliezer. You will represent Abraham at the Milah, and your presence will strengthen me at my task. I believe it will be of comfort to the twins when you hold them."

. . .

On the morning of the eighth day, before suckling the infants, Rebekah brings them to Isaac washed and wrapped in linens. Esau is fussy and fidgety. He is cranky and then begins to wail. Rebekah offers him her breast. He shoves it away. Rebekah knows he is not rejecting her. She feels like she is lacking something he needs to be calm and at peace. It frustrates her all the more when she remembers how nothing she did in her father's house could please Laban, her moody and domineering brother. Esau, in barely more than a week of life, reminds her of the oppressive past in Haran.

Rebekah places Esau on Eliezer's lap. She unwraps the linen, exposing the baby's generative tool. As soon as the air touches his parts, Esau's crying increases.

"Ho, little one," Eliezer smiles, "nobody has hurt you so far. Be brave."

Eliezer instructs Rebekah. "Insert your smallest finger's nail between Esau's foreskin and the tip of his penis to separate the two. Go all the way around the tip."

Isaac Unbound

When Rebekah completes this, to the squalling of Esau, whose face is redder than usual, Eliezer says to Isaac, "Pull the foreskin down and cut with the flint knife the part of the foreskin stretched beyond the tip of the penis. Do it quickly. Do not hesitate."

Isaac follows Eliezer's instructions. Eliezer says, "Esau, may you live and flourish as the firstborn through the blood of this Covenant."

Isaac replies, "May this be the will of Gevurah."

Rebekah swaddles Esau. He takes her breast like a ravenous wolf and shortly falls into a sound sleep.

Rebekah brings Jacob to Eliezer. The child is calm. He has a wan smile on his lips. His symmetrical features and olive complexion draw his parents and Eliezer to him. He is a tiny version of Isaac. When he furrows his brow and stares intently, he reminds them all of Abraham when he used to pray to El Shaddai.

Isaac circumcises his younger twin. Eliezer says, "Jacob, may you live and flourish as the father of tribes through the blood of this Covenant."

Isaac replies, "May this be the will of Gevurah."

Jacob barely whimpers through the cutting of the Covenant. Immediately after being swaddled, he sleeps peacefully. Whatever distance Rebekah feels from her firstborn, there is no question about her free-flowing, unconditional love for Jacob. She assumes the seed of maternal love for Esau will grow in time, but it remains a question hidden in her heart. It is not a question she is urgent to think about or to discuss with Isaac.

XVI

Wrestlings

As the twins grow in years and height, Rebekah misses their infancy and toddler days. She and Isaac have tried to bring more children into their family to no result. Isaac wonders about the divine promise to make Abraham and Sarah's descendants as numerous as the stars. He does not cease believing in Gevurah's pledge. He begins to understand that its realization will take many generations over many centuries.

When the boys are ten years old, Isaac summons them to his tent. They hurry to hear what Isaac wants of them. They enter his tent. He offers them cups of goat milk while their eyes adjust to the dim light inside the tent.

"My sons, it is time for you to learn the ways of earning a livelihood as shepherds and farmers. No longer will you occupy yourselves with children's games and wanderings."

"But, Father," Jacob says, "you don't work. You have all your servants under Eliezer's charge among the flocks and in the gardens. Why can't we use servants when we grow up?"

"Because, my son, you must first depend on yourself before depending on others."

"Father, you know I hate the intensity of the sun and the smell of the goats. Let me remain in my tent. I can braid thongs out of dried goat skin."

"This is not a choice for you. You must spend a year working outdoors, tending flocks and furrows."

"Father," Esau says, "I have been waiting for you to set us to grown-up work. I love being outside, being part of the world full of life. It makes me feel alive."

"The two of you will meet Baalartzi, Eliezer's chief Canaanite servant, at dawn tomorrow. He will train you in the ways of sustaining our clan. This knowledge may well save you someday and even enrich you."

The boys receive kisses on their heads from Isaac and depart his tent. Esau runs to Rebekah's tent. He is flushed with vigor and excitement when he encounters Rebekah leaving her tent.

"Mother, Father is setting us to work among the flocks and in the fields with Baalartzi tomorrow. We will learn this work for a year. I can't wait to start."

Esau begins to jump and twirl with excitement. His energy builds, bursting like an earthquake in the valley of the Jordan. In the year ahead, he will be in his favored element.

"This is truly good news, Esau. But I am going now to see how your brother is doing. Save your energy, for you will need it tomorrow and in the days to come."

Rebekah leaves. She leaves Esau wondering why she hardly listens to him. When he is excited to share an experience in the outdoors, it is as though she cannot be bothered. She has other things to do. He wishes she would kiss him on the head as Isaac does.

Rebekah walks the short distance to Jacob, who is sitting in front of his tent. He has a stick in his hand. He is drawing in the dirt. He creates buildings and houses like one sees in cities. He sketches a tower that stretches above the city, but the tower is not yet completed.

"Jacob, I understand your father has spoken to you about working with the goats and in the fields with Baalartzi."

"Yes, Mother. Father gives us no choice. Esau seems to be happy with the plan. I would prefer to sketch and dream about how we might build Canaan."

"Your father is concerned for your future and our clan's future. You must learn to make a livelihood, though I know you prefer other means to do so."

"If you know that, Mother, please speak to Father to get him to release me from the dreadful year I face. Please, Mother, please do something to get me more time in my tent than among the goats. Their bleating drives me crazy. My throat closes at their odor."

"Jacob, I cannot get your father to release you from the work. I too think you need to learn something of herding and farming. But I will offer you a deal. If you do your work with the animals and the earth without complaining or slacking, I will hire a teacher for you. He will teach you how to deal and trade. You will learn how to detect offers that seem good but will take advantage of you. You will become skilled in making offers that protect your interests and are fair. This will be vital knowledge beyond herding flocks. Our goats are wealth, but our wealth depends on knowing how to trade them."

"Mother, that really excites me. I would like to become skilled at trading. Who would teach me—Eliezer?"

"I will engage Itai, the grandson of Ephron the Hittite. When your grandfather Abraham bought the cave of Machpelah in the field of Ephron, the old Hittite drove a hard bargain. Itai can teach you about people, patience, and tough negotiation while keeping a gracious tone."

"Thank you, Mother. When may I start with Itai?"

"First, I must get your father to agree. I am sure he will go along with hiring Itai. But you must devote yourself for at least half a year to doing the work Isaac requires of you. During the second half year, we will have Itai teach you here each afternoon when you complete the day's work. Do you commit yourself to the work, Jacob?"

"Yes, Mother, I do."

Rebekah kisses Jacob on his head and goes off in the direction of Isaac's tent.

Isaac is meditating, as he does every afternoon. He concentrates on Gevurah's many blessings: having a wife who understands him and who is wise; being able to remain in Canaan and not go to Egypt as did Abraham; having two sons who will secure the family's future.

He considers his sons. Esau is physically strong, athletic, and bold. Isaac wishes he had those qualities. Esau is kind and compassionate as well. He will make an excellent leader of the tribe, not merely because he is the firstborn, but because of his personal qualities. Isaac desires that Esau experience Gevurah, have some sense of the holy. The boy is young yet, but Isaac hopes that if Esau seeks the divine, he will enter into relationship with Gevurah or with his own understanding of Being.

He sees that Jacob is more like himself. Jacob has a spiritual side. He too spends time in his tent in thought and prayer. He can be tough and strong when the occasion requires. There is also a clever side to Jacob. He casts a shadow, a mere suggestion, of being sly, conniving. Perhaps he will outgrow this trait, which he displayed even at birth, seeking to supplant Esau. He is also fortunate to have his mother's intense, unconditional love. Would that Rebekah loved Esau as mightily as she holds Jacob dear.

"My husband, forgive me for breaking into your meditations. I want to tell you of an agreement I made with Jacob that requires your approval and blessing."

Rebekah calls Isaac's attention to how difficult the year of working in flocks and fields will be for Jacob. He needs more mental exertion and something to quench his curiosity. She tells Isaac of her proposal that if Jacob commits himself to working diligently to meet Isaac's requirement, she will hire Itai the Hittite to teach Jacob buying and selling, trading, and bargaining. A gentle smile brushes Isaac's eyes.

"Rebekah, my sister, my bride, how precious you are to me. Again, you show your wisdom and your sensitive nature. I support your plan for Jacob. It has my blessing. If Itai can teach Jacob even a tenth of his skills, Jacob will do well in his day."

"Thank you, Isaac. I will let Jacob know of your blessing."

"Rebekah, there is another matter on my mind."

"Please speak your mind to me, Isaac, as we always have to each other."

"Rebekah, I am saddened and concerned. You seem to favor Jacob with your attention and love. I think Esau senses your distance, a certain absence of your heart. I try to make up the love to him that he misses from you. Am I wrong? Am I imagining this?"

"Isaac, you are not entirely wrong in what you see and what you sense. Of course I love Esau. He is my firstborn. But he doesn't need me as Jacob needs me. Esau is strong. As an infant, he would often push me away. I know it is not his fault that he is the image physically of his uncle, my brother, Laban. But his face reminds me of how Laban abused me and took advantage of me. I repeatedly tell myself Esau is not Laban, but somehow the chill in my heart makes me absent to Esau. Jacob wants me close to him. He hugs me and smiles at me with the same brightness as your smile. I need to give all of myself to him, and it is easy to do."

"Rebekah, do you see that Jacob, who grasped Esau's heel during their birth, is still doing so? He may not be aware of supplanting your love for Esau. You may not see this, but that is what seems to have happened. Can you perhaps give Esau more of your maternal tenderness and care? My love, to compensate him, cannot touch him as deeply as his mother's love."

"I will try, Isaac, to be more loving and attentive to Esau. He does have a kind heart. I know he is not my brother Laban. It's just that when I am with Jacob, he reflects your looks and the best aspects of your spirit. I will try to be more available to Esau. On the other hand, Isaac, I say that it would be well for you to spend more time with Jacob."

"Just because Jacob is so like me and has a spiritual sense, I feel he needs me less than Esau does. Esau requires instruction about the divine light that shines on our clan. He is young yet. I hope his heart will expand to search for Gevurah. As leader of our clan in the future, Esau will need to commit to our Covenant. I will make a larger effort to engage him in learning about our clan, our God, and our Covenant."

"Isaac, this conversation leads me to tell you something I have kept from you for over nine years, since I was pregnant with the twins. I was late into my pregnancy. The boys were wrestling around in my womb, barely quieting down. Their movement not only caused me pain but worried me as well. Such vigorous tumbling and struggling did not seem normal to me. I was visiting Abraham in his tent. He looked at me and saw that I was wan and downhearted. He asked what was wrong with me since I was not cheerful. When I told him of what felt like a wrestling contest going on inside me, Abraham asked if he could place his hand on my womb. I allowed him to do so. He was gentle when he put his hand on me. He was patient, letting the sensation of the children's movement penetrate his heart. He spoke after a while, telling me I was pregnant with twins. He said each would become a nation in his own right. He also said the elder would serve the younger."

"What are you telling me, Rebekah? Esau is our firstborn. I expect he will lead this clan when I am sleeping in Machpelah. For that reason, I take Esau to me to teach him our ways, to guide him."

"Isaac, I merely share with you what Abraham foresaw. Perhaps his prophecy can give you direction as you teach our sons."

"Rebekah, would you have me take Esau up Mount Moriah to slay his rights as firstborn? There will be no shattering, no slaughtering, and no shards in this generation. Abraham, in his last days, would try to control this clan. That will not happen. Neither Gevurah nor I will permit the rights of the firstborn to be stripped from Esau. Now, please go, and send Esau to me."

Esau comes in from the fields to Isaac.

"Father, I have been toiling in the furrows as you directed. My hands are blistered, and my back aches from the work."

"This labor will strengthen you, my son. Your hands will, in time, be as tough as leather, and your young back will become as flexible as a willow branch. I have called you to me now to talk about something other than your field work. We need to talk about Gevurah and the divine Covenant with our clan."

"Father, such talk makes my head spin. It makes me dizzy. Why must we have this talk now. There will be time when I am older."

"Esau, you are my firstborn. You are to be the leader of our clan after my death. In order to fulfill your responsibility and receive that privilege, you must know something of the ways of Gevurah and what the Covenant means. It will be up to you to teach the clan so they may share in the Covenant. I want to teach you my understanding and tell you of Abraham's views. They are not the same, though parts are connected. You will need to form your own ideas, but you must build on the platform of the thoughts and experiences of your parents and grandparents."

"Father, I respect what you say to me, but this is not what I wish to learn now. I need to know how to live in this world. I do not want to herd goats or be a farmer. I seek a different way."

"What would you do in your life, Esau?"

"Father, I wish to become a skilled hunter. I want to be in the wild, in the hills and plains, hunting prey to nourish the clan. Let me learn and practice this skill now. I will attend to Gevurah and the Covenant at a later time."

"Esau, if it is your desire to become a skilled hunter, I will send you to live and learn with your uncle Ishmael at Be'er LaChai Ro'i in Paran. He is an able hunter and a man of might. I will have Eliezer tell Ishmael you will be visiting when the time comes. I do have three things to ask of you. The first is that you will complete this year with the flocks and the fields, just as Jacob must do. Secondly, I want you to ask Ishmael about his God, Chai Ro'i, and his experience of his God. My third request is this: when you complete your time learning to hunt from your uncle, hunt for me a gazelle from the mountains near Yevus. Come home and make me a stew of that game. I love it and yearn for it. That dish renews my spirit."

"Father, I will do everything you ask of me, beginning next year with Ishmael."

"Very good, my son. Go back to the fields with my blessing."

XVII

Differences and Distances

It has been six months since Jacob and Esau began shepherding the goats and laboring in the grain fields. Jacob's skin is leathery, dark, and burnished from long days in the sun. He is stronger now and bulking up with muscle. But, for Jacob, the work remains drudgery replete with repetitive dullness. If only he could think great thoughts with clarity while following the goats. Unrelenting sun and blasting winds from the eastern desert distract him from the flow of his mind's meanderings. So it is when Itai the Hittite enters the camp one evening in the summer month of Av that Jacob's ennui becomes elation.

Rebecca greets Itai the Hittite, whom she has personally hired. She brings him to Jacob, who is standing among the goats grazing on sparse yellowed weeds among rocks and boulders.

"My son, come meet Itai. He is here now to teach you bartering and trading, negotiating and selling, just as you asked. You will complete your work in fields and on hillsides each day, but the last two hours of daylight will be yours to spend learning from Itai."

"Thank you, Mother. Welcome, Itai. I am very happy you are here. Give me time to corral the goats, and I'll be ready to learn."

When Isaac becomes aware of Itai's presence in the camp, he goes out to the melon field, where Esau is working. He calls to Esau from the edge of the partially harvested field.

DIFFERENCES AND DISTANCES

"Esau, come here."

Esau strides over to his father. Isaac marvels at Esau's ebullient mood and determined gait. Unquestionably, work in the outdoors is like drinking new wine for Esau. He is quenched and full of energy.

"Esau, your brother's tutor, Itai, arrived today. That means Jacob will work outside less in order to learn from him. It also tells me it is time to send you to your uncle Ishmael to learn from him the secrets of the hunt. Pack your clothes and provisions. Go to Ishmael and listen well to his words."

"Who will accompany me, Father?"

"My son, the path is safe, and you have grown large. None will fool with you. You will take a donkey and traverse the wilderness to the tents of Ishmael."

The following morning, Esau sets out for Ishmael's camp at the oasis of Be'er Lachai Ro'i in the Wilderness of Paran. When he arrives on the third afternoon, two of his cousins, Kedar and Hadad, warmly greet him. They take Esau to their father, Ishmael.

"Esau, welcome to my home. Your father, my dear brother Isaac, sent Eliezer to me. He told me of your desire to become a hunter and caravan raider."

"Uncle, I want very much to learn to hunt. I love being in the mountains and on the plains, and I value the idea of providing for my family a diet beyond goat meat. As for raiding caravans, I am not so interested. We must keep peaceful relations with other Canaanites in the land."

"I understand, Esau. Hunting lessons we will have then."

Esau remains with Ishmael for six months. Esau learns to bend a long, sturdy branch after immersing it in water to make a bow. He becomes adept at carving arrows and tying on bronze points. Each day, Ishmael takes Esau to practice shooting. He emphasizes to Esau the need to focus his mind, to shut out distractions. He teaches Esau to take measured, even breaths. The biggest challenge is mastering the arm strength to pull back the bow string to the apex of its arc, then to relax shoulder and hand to release the missile.

"Esau, when I hunt, I always concentrate on the life of the creature. I consider that the animal has a right to its life, though we take it that we may live ourselves. So it is that before I release my arrow, I try to make eye contact with my target as I whisper a word of thanks. I feel I need to convey my gratitude in exchange for its life force. I am also paying close attention to the beast's heart. I want to direct my arrow there in order to bring a quick death with minimal suffering. All this can be accomplished if you focus your mind, gird your attention, and hunt with humility. This means if other matters distract you and divert your attention, it is not a day for you to hunt."

"Uncle Ishmael, I will hold tight to your lessons. They speak to my heart. If it is possible to shed blood without stripping away swaths of my caring for animals and nature, I will feel whole."

"You should know, Esau, that there is one other act I perform as part of my hunting. After I shoot a creature through its heart and it is dead, I cut its neck and sever its veins. I hang it from a branch facedown until its blood drips out onto the ground. Then, I cover its blood with earth."

"That is amazing, Uncle. All the tribes in the Canaanite hill country think animal blood is a delicacy to make one strong. They make soup from the blood or mix it with flour to make porridge."

"I am not a Canaanite, Esau. My mother, Hagar, is Egyptian. Your father, Isaac, sees himself as a Canaanite, yet he refrains from consuming the blood of the hunted creature or of his domestic goats and sheep. He believes his Covenant with his God, Gevurah, prohibits him from eating blood. I think this abstinence relates to cultivating and furthering one's compassion and sensitivity to the value of all life."

"I am considering all your teachings, Uncle. It is clear that hunting, even for sustenance, is not a mere matter of taking life. I see that if I follow carefully your guiding counsel, there may be days when my hunt will lack a successful result. Even at that, I will have been in the open spaces and mountains, which I love."

After six months, Ishmael tells Esau, "You have absorbed my teaching, Nephew. Go back to your father tomorrow. Tell him

Differences and Distances

I said you have learned well. You may relay to Isaac that I think you have the heart of a hunter, which reflects the compassion of Gevurah."

Jacob has also completed his months of tutelage with Itai the Hittite. Itai has taught him many ways to read others. Look at the eyebrows, the forehead, the mouth, and the limbs. They will tell you of the true mind and heart. If you can read these, you will know with whom you are dealing and what kind of bargain you may make. You will understand whether or not to offer a deal first and just what an obtainable goal is. Itai has shown Jacob how to speak in a grand, ingratiating way in order to bait the hook of trust in a big fish who wants to trade or to do business with him. Itai has told Jacob always to ask for substantially more than what you think something is worth or what your interlocutor can likely afford. That way, you can assure making a substantial profit while flattering the bargainer. Further, try to evaluate how badly he wishes what you are selling or trading and set a price accordingly.

"Jacob," Itai says, "if you follow my guidance, you will most often do well and prevail. That is what happened when your grandfather, Abraham, bargained with my grandfather, Effron, for the Machpelah cave. Effron could see how urgent it was for Abraham to acquire a burial site. My grandfather sought no less than two hundred shekels, but he did not quote this price to Abraham. He doubled that amount to four hundred shekels, and that was the price he received. He recognized that Abraham was sorely in need of a burial place for his wife. He was aware that Abraham was wealthy and blessed with everything. Effron read Abraham correctly and ended up with a comely income from the sale. Abraham was certain he had gotten a fair price for a choice holding."

Itai leaves Jacob with one more principle. It does not seem obvious at first. He tells Jacob, "Always opt for the less precious commodity because it will become either more available or more valuable. Choose bronze over gold and iron. Bronze is more plentiful and easily acquired. Iron and gold are valued but harder to obtain. Bronze has become used for mirrors and for decorative purposes. It is in demand by many, while gold and iron's use is more limited. Agree to accept a dozen speckled and spotted goats over three pure white ones. You will always come out on top by following this principle."

Jacob and Esau complete their tutorials, which provide a foundation on which to build their adult lives. Each set of lessons matches well elements of their natures and personalities. Those lessons will mold and influence their choices and behaviors as their years progress. Now, they are both at home in the camp of Isaac and Rebekah in Be'er Sheva. Both do a small amount of shepherding and farming, but those are mostly the tasks of slaves. Jacob conducts trading with other Canaanites and foreign merchants. Esau hunts as much as three days a week to expand the palate and eating enjoyment of the clan. Each of them wants to gain parental approval. Jacob revels in his mother's love. She sees that he is quite clever and cunning. Esau is aware he lacks her maternal devotion, so he remains close to Isaac, who wishes to compensate his first-born but whose efforts are limping if not feeble. The division between Esau and Jacob, which began in childhood as a minute crack in the ground of their family life, has now widened to a gully's width and is moving toward becoming a deep and stretched-out chasm.

XVIII

Searching

SOME TIME FOLLOWING THESE events, Isaac goes out to the field to meditate as the day descends towards dusk. He is unsettled because Esau, his sixteen-year-old firstborn son, does not seem to be on the path of the Covenant. He is not inclined to discuss his father's God, Gevurah. Isaac, in some measure, blames himself for not teaching Esau in his younger years the foundations of the Covenant. Isaac reflects that he took too little initiative in order to avoid reprising Abraham's rigid and oppressive devotion to El Shaddai.

Esau is also too familiar with the local Canaanite clans. He visits them regularly. He engages in contests of strength and skill with them. Isaac worries it will be only a matter of time until Esau joins his Canaanite friends to attend Baal worship or Astarte feasts. What if, Isaac muses, Esau takes a Canaanite wife? He is always flirting with Canaanite girls, who entice him to the threshing floor. Isaac cannot imagine Esau would follow the Covenant if he married out of the Hebrew tribe.

Isaac looks up and sees Esau coming in his direction from the fields. He wants to engage his son, to talk about Gevurah and the Covenant. Before Isaac says a word, Esau greets him.

"Father, a good evening to you. Are you well?"

"I am well, my son, thanks to the protection and generous care of Gevurah. It is that care and its source that I have been wanting to discuss with you."

"Father, I don't think of such matters very much. What I do think about is how I can be a kind and caring son to you and Mother, though she seems not to pay attention. If part of my love for you can be expressed by listening to what you wish to teach me about Gevurah, I will do so. But, first, I would begin by hunting the Yevus gazelle and cooking the stew of your heart's desire. We can talk about things over a meal of gazelle stew."

"Very well, Esau. I look forward to sharing my favorite dish if Gevurah gives you favor and success in your hunt. Only I ask you not to be gone too many days. You are needed at home as well."

"I will leave in the morning and be back in no more than three days."

"Go in peace, my son."

Esau leaves at early light. He heads northeast to the hills of Yevus. Those mountains in late spring are usually covered with thick and verdant grasses. They embody a song of fertility in their being as they reach upward to the heavens. Among the grasses are tiny wise men with flowing robes and conical hats—the mushrooms of the Yevus hills. They beckon to be picked, cooked, and savored in stew. Every few steps, pink anemones and red and white bowing cyclamen adorn the slopes. That is how Esau recalls the life in these hills each year in late spring.

Now, as Esau starts his ascent into the hills and mountains, the yellow, desiccated grasses, absent of mushrooms and flowers, shock him. He knows the plains, not to mention the lands of the northern desert at Be'er Sheva, have received less rain recently than in other winters. Yet he has hoped that the wisps of clouds that blew over the land from the Great Sea would coalesce, chill, and release their moisture over the hills. That would provide a measure of sustenance for gazelle and rock conies, as well as for ravenous wolves and lions who depend on them.

As Esau starts to doubt that he will have any gazelles to bring home, he counsels himself to be patient. He has another day in the hills until he must be home and in his father's tent. He roams the hills. He seeks springs and streams that may yet exist and would be gathering places for animals.

There are no flowing rivulets, only dry beds whose courses remind him of wetter days.

Esau makes his way through the hills with a deliberate and quiet gait, alert, his eyes roving, seeking animal movement. Then, just beyond a clump of pines, he spies a young gazelle grazing among the meager grass around the trees. The gazelle looks up and makes fluttering eye contact with Esau. The hunter's bronze-tipped arrow is on the bowstring. As he draws back the arrow in the bow, a lion leaps from the thicket and snatches the gazelle from behind. The arrow misses. Esau looks for it in the brush. He has lost it and the gazelle he wished so much to bring home.

By the end of the day, Esau is discouraged and disappointed. He opens the rolled goat skins he had packed, eats a few fistfuls of parched grain, and lies down to pass the night with sleep.

Only he cannot fall asleep. It is neither the howling of jackals nor the rooting and snorting of wild boars that prevent his sleep. The thought he has banished from his heart now returns as darkness surrounds him.

"Mother does not care for me. She speaks sparingly to me when it is impossible for her to avoid me. I cannot fathom why she does not express love to me as she does for Jacob. As much as Father tries to make up for Mother's coldness, he cannot fill the void I feel within. I try to be kind, loving, and respectful to Mother. I do for her the tasks and favors she asks. My efforts seem to bounce off her, reminiscent of bronze-tipped arrows deflected by an iron shield. Perhaps it is time for me to speak directly to her or to Father so that I might understand and possibly overcome her pushing me away. Let me see what I am able to do when I return home. All I know is that home feels to me like a broken place. Would that I could find ways to plaster the cracks with care and connect the shards through shared and honest conversation."

Esau finally lets go of this struggle and sleeps a fitful slumber until the sky lightens. He is hungry and eats the parched grain he can barely tolerate. His revulsion by it will not be a problem because he has finished what he brought. Between his provisions running out and the scarcity of game, he will journey home with an empty stomach, growing exhaustion, and a quiver full of arrows that did not attain their purpose.

As a result, he is unclear about the direction from which he came. He is dizzy, and instead of walking with his confident steps, he stumbles off on the wrong path. Hours go by as Esau meanders around the hills. Hunger intensifies, and his thinking is dull. He looks at the risen sun, which is now fully in the sky. He calculates the southwesterly path he will need to get back to Be'er Sheva.

He devotes the rest of the day's light to walking home with weak and uncertain steps. By midafternoon, he reaches his family's camp at Be'er Sheva. It is inactive, peaceful, as people rest in their tents during the height of the sun's intensity. As Esau enters the camp, he is ravenous. He looks for cooking fires over which pots hang with food. None. There are none from which to ladle the porridge or meager stew. Any of the clan would gladly feed Esau, but mealtime has ended. As Esau turns away, downhearted and with his stomach rumbling, he sees smoke and a fire in a circle of rocks outside Jacob's tent. Perhaps his brother will have something to share from the pot hanging over the fire. Esau heads off to Jacob's tent and the campfire in front of it.

XIX

Guile and Guilt

JACOB IS IN HIS tent, thinking about the conversation Rebekah had opened with him yesterday. Rebekah had come to his tent. She seemed burdened. Soon, she told him what was weighing on her heart.

"Jacob, I want to talk to you about your father and your brother."

"Yes, Mother, I am listening."

"Have you noticed how your father is weakening?"

"What are you referring to, Mother?"

"Isaac is having trouble seeing. He trips frequently on objects. While he usually catches himself, he falls occasionally. But he won't admit to problems with his vision."

"I agree that his sight is weakening. On the few occasions I've hinted to him that he seems to have a problem seeing, he waves away the subject with uncharacteristic impatience."

"It is uncharacteristic of your father. If anything, he's always been slow to anger, accepting, and quick to forgive. I see those traits in the way Isaac relates to your brother."

"Father loves Esau dearly. What are you referring to, Mother?"

"He does not press Esau to discuss ideas of the divine or to delve into the requirements of the Covenant. Esau resists conversing in that realm, and your father lets it pass. Isaac is patient, though I know such a conversation is uppermost in his mind. On some level, it is as though your father is wrestling with what he knows Esau must engage. On another level, he seems to accept that Esau is a man of the fields and of the hunt, not a family patriarch with all it entails."

"Do you think Father notices Esau's involvement with neighboring Canaanite young women?"

"Despite his failing sight, his hearing is still acute. He hears the laughter and teasing your brother conducts with the girls. He knows your brother runs into the vineyards at the fall harvest ingathering to let the women chase him. He suspects Esau lets one of them catch him and that they raise each other's skirts."

"If Esau ends up marrying one of them, there is little hope of maintaining Gevurah's Covenant. The enticement and influence of her Canaanite family would erase the vales of our small Hebrew Canaanite clan."

"Jacob, I believe the only answer is for your father to send Esau to my family in Haran so that he may bring back a wife from there, just as I was brought to Canaan."

"You know that Father can hardly stand a few days apart from Esau when he is hunting. It is not likely he will tolerate the idea of Esau being away for many months. At least when Grandfather Abraham sought a wife for Father, it was Eliezer who went to Haran. Now that Eliezer sleeps with his ancestors, who could go but Esau himself?"

"Jacob, you are so astute and wise. Please think about how we might influence Isaac so he may properly guide Esau on these matters."

"I will give it some thought, Mother, but I ask you to be realistic. I am not certain there is much I can do. Father may feel disrespected if I enter this realm directly."

"Yes, caution is called for, but consider if there is some way you might grasp Esau's heel with subtlety and cunning."

"What are you suggesting, Mother?"

"That our clan needs you to be its chief after Isaac passes."

Jacob is struck mute by his mother's words as she leaves his tent. He is the younger son by but a few minutes. Yet those brief moments established Esau's ultimate authority over him and the clan for years to come. Even the family myth of Jacob's grabbing Esau's heel at their birth cannot suggest that a symbolic grasping will supplant Esau's birthright. Such a thought had never previously occurred to Jacob.

Today, a day after his exchange with Rebekah, Jacob sits near his fire. He intermittently stirs a pot of red lentils he has been cooking slowly since this morning. Through the smoke, Jacob sees Esau coming toward him. He is ragged and disheveled, his hair matted, his steps stumbling and unsure as though he had drunk much wine. There is no gazelle carcass across his back, whose presence would boast of a successful hunt.

Jacob gets up and puts Esau's arm around his shoulder as a support for him. Esau breathes heavily. He is exhausted. Jacob eases him to the ground near the fire.

"Esau, I see your hunt did not produce results, though you were gone for days. I am sorry for you and for Father, who longs for gazelle stew. May you have better fortune next time you go out."

"Jacob, I need food. I need it now. I am ravenous. Give me some of your red, red lentils."

"Certainly, Brother, but rest yourself for a bit. Catch your breath. Let me stir the lentils."

Esau has no strength. Urgent is his hunger. Jacob stirs the lentils and observes Esau. His back is bent, and his shoulders are hunched. He releases a tear from each eye. He does not look like the mighty hunter. He hardly seems a future leader of a tribe, much less a Covenant-bearer.

"Jacob, enough stirring of the red stuff. Give me a bowl of it, now."

Seeing Esau in his needy and weakened state, Jacob feels pity for his brother. He also remembers yesterday's conversation with his mother. As Jacob looks upon Esau's incapacity and desperate need of food, an idea unbidden comes into his mind. He remembers the lessons he learned from Itai the Hittite. He gives Esau a bowl with a small portion of lentils.

"Esau, taste this. If it pleases your palate, I will give you more."

Esau consumes the lentils and says, "Give me a full bowl now!"

Jacob replies, "It is my duty as your brother to feed you, but perhaps in appreciation, you will give me your birthright in exchange for the lentils."

"Birthright? What are you talking about, Jacob?"

"Esau, you must know as the elder brother, Isaac's firstborn, that you will become our clan's chief when Father is laid to rest in the cave of Machpelah. Are you clear about assuming such leadership? Do you know what will be required of you?"

"All I know, Jacob, is that I am beyond being faint with hunger. I feel like death is near. So, if I were to die, what good is my birthright? If I die, you will inherit the birthright in any case. So take it. I give it to you. Now give me the lentils."

"First, swear to me that you give me your birthright now."

"I swear, Jacob."

Jacob serves Esau a full bowl of steaming red lentils. Esau devours it, gulps down a goat skin of water, releases a thunderous belch, gets up, and goes to his tent.

A flutter of guilt enters Jacob's heart for trapping Esau and tricking him out of his birthright. His guilt is quickly assuaged by his memory of Rebekah's words regarding Esau as unfit to lead. Jacob will be head of the Hebrew tribe in years to come. He realizes that his father cannot know that he has grasped and taken Esau's birthright by trickery. He must talk further with Esau.

In the morning, Jacob stands outside Esau's tent and calls him. Esau comes out. He looks rested and alert. It is as though the dust of his despair rolled away when he rinsed the grime of field and forest from his skin.

"What more do you want from me, Jacob? You fulfilled your intention to squeeze me into giving up my birthright. I have nothing further to yield up for your benefit."

"I only want to suggest to you it would be prudent as well as kind of you to refrain from telling Father you exchanged your birthright for a bowl of lentils. That would crush his spirit. He would be angry. He would be disappointed and perhaps not so forgiving."

"Jacob, I have already decided not to share our bargain with Father, but I must tell you that no matter your reasons, you did not behave toward me in a brotherly way."

"Look, Esau, if you did not like my offer or if you felt more strongly about keeping your birthright, you could have left my fire and my tent to seek sustenance from another in our camp."

"You took advantage of my weakened state and my loss of heart. I guess you learned well the lessons taught you by Itai, grandson of Ephron the Hittite. Is this skill of bending back the fingers, so to speak, of one already in supplication a point of pride for you?"

"I did what I thought was necessary to preserve our clan and our Covenant with Gevurah."

Jacob returns to his tent. Esau turns toward the nearby pasture land. Esau muses on how Jacob and even Rebekah have misread him. They think he is dull-witted and plodding. They are quite sure he is an insensitive dolt. They have not observed his attentions to his father. They have discounted his care for their flocks and fields. A hunter must be a clever planner, aware of nuances in the natural world, and stealthy. Esau knows in his heart he possesses these traits. He knows that only the paternal blessing of the firstborn secures and confirms the birthright. He has every intention, at the appropriate time, of receiving the paternal blessing and snatching back the birthright Jacob has seized by guile.

XX

Opening the Eyes of the Blind

AS THE TWINS REACH their seventeenth year, Esau brings two women as his wives into the camp of Isaac and Rebekah. Both are daughters of Hittites who live in Canaan. The senior wife is Judith bat Be'eri. The second wife is Basemat bat Elon. The two women are respectful and attentive to Isaac and Rebekah. They speak kindly. They assist Esau in the fields and continue that work when he is hunting. Judith plays the shepherd's flute, and Basemat sings songs of Canaan with a lilting, sweet voice. It seems Esau has brought to the camp beautiful women who are as flexible as desert willows following a rain.

With all of the generous heart they bring to the tents of Esau, Isaac and Rebekah are not warmed by their presence. Judith and Basemat have brought from their family homes statues of Astarte, the fertility goddess who is the consort of Ba'al, the god of thunder. Esau had told them before they joined him at Be'er Sheva not to bring images of their gods and goddesses into his camp. He had warned them of the extreme upset the presence of those gods would cause Isaac. Esau had explained that Isaac's God is Gevurah, the mighty singular deity who creates all beings, who is above nature itself, and who unifies all life. He had told his wives that Gevurah is beyond all existing things and cannot be imagined or represented by any created being.

The wives cannot grasp a god who is not within nature and whose face and presence cannot be shaped into clay or stone. Esau tells them that if it were up to him, he could not care less what gods they worship. He is neither partial to Gevurah nor to his grandfather's God, El Shaddai. What does bother him are their frequent references to their gods. If it is Basemat's turn to lie with Esau on a given night, Judith bids her goodnight, saying aloud, "May Astarte grant you fruit this night." After a dry spell in winter, Basemat prays with Judith, "O Ba'al, grant rain to the land, impregnate the soil with your divine seed."

They say such words in the hearing of Isaac and Rebekah. It brings Esau's parents bitterness of heart and spirit. These aging clan parents wonder whether their way of life will have a distinct presence and a role in the land. Will the family, with its special focus on walking with Gevurah in righteousness, be swept away by the Canaanite attachment to Ba'al and Astarte? Have they endured various trials and painful family tempests only to be overwhelmed by the Canaanite ways? These questions fill the hearts of Isaac and Rebekah. The answers seem to be unpromising for the future, filling them with despair.

After months of wrestling within her heart over this situation, Rebekah draws on her inner well of strength. She goes to Isaac's tent. She enters without a word.

"Who is there?" Isaac asks after his dozing is interrupted.

"It is me, my husband. Your eyes seem to be growing more dim."

"Yes Rebekah, my eyes are beclouded, and I am left with only shadowy impressions. Tell me now, my wife, what is on your mind."

"Judith and Baseman are leading Esau ever farther from Gevurah and our Covenant with the divine. How will our clan flourish without Gevurah's sustaining presence if we don't uphold our commitments and responsibilities?"

"What would you have me do, Rebekah? Esau is our firstborn. He is a precious son to me. I can't simply refuse him his birthright. I won't exile him as Ishmael was exiled. I won't reduce his stature by sacrificing his position."

"Isaac, despite our partnership in Gevurah's Covenant, I know it is not my place to tell you what to do. Give Jacob your paternal blessing. Confirm him in the birthright Esau sold him for a bowl of lentils."

"Esau sold Jacob his birthright? I was never told of this. Surely it must have been in a moment of weakness. Jacob is wily enough to size up and take advantage of a situation. But Esau must know that his yielding of his birthright will be invalid once I give him my blessing."

"Please, Isaac, I implore you to do what's right to preserve our future. Give your blessing to Jacob."

"I will never intentionally hurt or crush my Esau. Rebekah, you must trust that Gevurah will sustain us as a faithful people at this time and into the future. Now, please get my walking stick and lead me to the edge of the field, where I can think and meditate."

Isaac is left alone. He sits on a boulder on the field's border. He breathes in the enchanting scents of soil and stalks of wheat. His feet tell him how dry and cracked the ground is. It has not rained in a few weeks. Since talking with Rebekah, the mosaic of cracked mud at his feet reflects to him his family's dilemma.

Isaac knows for certain that Esau is not the one who is fit to bear the Covenant for future generations. He became aware of this when Esau confessed to him that he sold his birthright to Jacob for a bowl of lentils. At the time, he did not reprimand or chastise Esau. He said nothing to Rebekah or to Jacob about the sale of the birthright. He reserved the right to bless Esau, thereby restoring to him the birthright. Isaac decided to watch and wait. As time passed and Esau brought Judith and Basemat into their clan's camp, Isaac came to know what he must do. He did not need Rebekah to tell him. The challenge is to find a way to avoid granting his blessing to Esau and to bestow it on Jacob. Isaac knows well that despite Esau's gruffness, he is a sensitive soul. Isaac commits himself to finding a way to deny the birthright blessing to Esau while not appearing to be culpable. There is no hurry to determine a path nor to rush down a rash course. He needs time to think and to plan with care.

Isaac hears the voice of someone in the field in its furthest furrow. It is the voice of Esau, and Isaac calls to him. "Esau, come; I need you!"

Esau does not like to keep his father waiting. He hurries toward Isaac. Isaac turns a quarter turn, leaning forward as though searching for his son.

"Here, Father; I am here." Esau gently touches Isaac's knee.

"Esau, please take me to my tent."

Esau leads Isaac to his tent and seats him in a wooden chair covered with soft goat skins. It is Isaac's favorite seat. Once Isaac is settled and comfortable, Esau asks if there is anything else Isaac requires.

"There is something more you can do. Go tell your mother that I want to speak with you privately and that we would appreciate her bringing us a tray of dried fruit and nuts."

Esau goes to Rebekah with Isaac's request. "Esau, do you have an idea what you father wishes to discuss with you?"

"No, Mother. It may be about our fields and the lack of substantial rain. Or, a more difficult and painful subject might be Father's unhappiness with Judith and Basemat. I really don't have a clear idea, but I am always ready to hear him and to learn from him."

"Go back to your father. I will shortly bring the tray of refreshments he requested. I know you both love the time you spend in one another's company."

Esau returns to Isaac's tent and takes the chair facing his father. Between them is a small table with inlaid wood of different shades.

"Esau, after Rebekah comes with the refreshment, I will tell you what's on my mind. I just don't want to be interrupted by her entrance. While we wait for her, would you mind lighting a few oil lamps? It seems very dim in here."

"Yes, Father. I am sorry to learn that your vision has gotten worse."

"I can barely make out the shape of your face and cannot see your features. We praise Gevurah for opening the eyes of the blind, and I would welcome such a miracle. Yet, I have come to realize this praise is not literally about physical blindness or about our eyes. Perhaps I should say it is about our inner sight. Gevurah should be praised for helping us see what we did not wish to see or were not able to see through the blinders of our favoritism or bias. I affirm that if we keep our spiritual eyes open, we will see into ourselves with depth and better understand the other person whom we see in front of us. We will know with clarity what to do and how to be."

Rebekah, holding the tray, enters the doorway of the tent. She sets the tray on the wooden table between her husband and son.

"I wish you both a good and useful conversation. Call me if you need anything more."

"Blessings upon you, Rebekah."

Rebekah leaves Isaac's tent. Neither Isaac nor Esau knows that she goes around to the back of the tent, where saddle bags are piled. Rebekah moves a few of the bags to make a cozy, cave-like space. Anyone passing the back of the tent, which rarely happens, would not notice Rebekah. It is not easy for a woman of her age to crouch on the ground. But she is determined to listen and anxious to hear what Isaac presents to Esau. This is what Rebekah hears Isaac say:

"My son, you are very dear to me. Never forget that I love you more than my own soul. Never forget my words to you, no matter what befalls you in your life. I love you.

"Esau, as you know, my eyes grow dim. Life becomes harder for me to get around. One day, perhaps not even so far in the future, Gevurah will summon me and call me to sleep with my father at Machpelah. Since none of us can know when he will be taken, a wise father makes preparation."

"Father, I am sure you have much time left. It pains me to think of your death. I can barely stand the fact of your increasing blindness. I remember the days of your vigor."

"Esau, it is time to face reality. That is as much your duty as it is my responsibility. This is what I would like you to do for me. Go to the mountains of Yevus and hunt for me a gazelle. Make from it my favorite stew. After I have partaken of your delectable stew and enjoyed some wine, I will bless you with my fatherly blessing. You will then become the leader of our clan. My blessing will confirm your birthright, which Jacob tricked away from you."

"Since Jacob took advantage of my weak position and stole my birthright, I have looked forward to receiving your blessing. That will make everything right. I will leave this very day for the mountains of Yevus."

"Come, kiss me, my son."

Isaac has always been captivated by the distinct scent of soil and sweat on Esau's skin.

Esau arises, kisses Isaac, his father, and departs the tent. Rebekah stays in her place behind Isaac's tent for some time. Then she enters Isaac's tent to fetch the tray.

"I hope your time with Esau was good and helpful."

"If Gevurah stands by his side and gives him a successful hunt, it will be well."

XXI

A Stew of Blessing

When Rebekah considers what she has heard Isaac say to Esau inside her husband's tent, she is convinced that Gevurah has opened a door for her to act. She now has the insight to do what is necessary to secure the clan and the Covenant. Necessity rests on a foundation of risk and boldness. It pains her to deceive and manipulate Isaac. The voice in her mind bolsters her resolve. It tells her that she must take steps to overcome Isaac's blind and unconditional love for Esau.

Rebekah makes sure no one witnesses her leaving the back of Isaac's tent. She walks with calm and deliberate steps to her tent. On the way, she passes Jacob's tent. Jacob is coming out to take his turn today in the goat pen.

"Ah, my son, I was just about to invite you to my tent."

"But, Mother, you know I have to take care of the goats and pasture them today. Can't we visit later?"

"No, Jacob. I need to speak with you now. Have a servant stand in for you with the goats. Please go to the pen and pick a choice kid. Bring it to my tent."

Jacob does as Rebekah asks. In a short while, he comes to her tent with a kid tethered on a rope.

"Please slaughter the kid, Jacob. Cut it up and bring me the pieces. I will make a stew of it for your father."

A Stew of Blessing

Jacob draws his knife across the throat of the unsuspecting kid. He uses the tether to tie together the rear legs of the animal. He hoists the other end of the tether over the acacia tree branch and pulls the kid off the ground. He waits until its blood finishes dripping onto the earth. Then he carves the flesh and brings it to Rebekah.

Jacob asks Rebekah, "Mother, what is the occasion that you are making goat stew this day?"

"This is the day when you will receive the birthright blessing from your father. When you are blessed, the clan and the Covenant will be placed securely in your hands."

"Mother, will you tell me how it is that you think I will receive Father's blessing today?"

"I heard your father instruct Esau to hunt a Yevus gazelle, bring it back to make a stew—his favorite dish—and then receive the birthright blessing. Esau has already left for Yevus. When the stew I am cooking is ready, you must go and sit with Isaac as he eats it, and then receive his blessing. That will confirm your possession of the birthright."

"Mother, you are putting me at risk of being cursed by Father if he senses it is I bringing the stew. Your plan is dangerous. It could destroy our clan. When Esau finds out, I can imagine he will resolve to kill me."

"Your father's blindness will protect you. Esau will not harm you while Isaac is alive, and it is likely he will let it go. He loves his life in the fields and with his Canaanite wives more than he cares about the birthright blessing."

"Even father's blindness will not secure for me his blessing. My voice—it is not like gravel as is my brother's voice. I am smoother, less hairy than Esau. What if Father touches me?"

"You will wear Esau's garments and goat skins when you go into his tents. We will put the goat skins on your neck so you will seem bearded and hirsute to Isaac. Jacob, this is what is required of you as our future leader. If anything should go wrong, I will take responsibility. I will take upon me and on my soul whatever curse may come from Isaac's lips. This is my oath to you."

Isaac Unbound

The stew and fresh bread cook until the sun is on the western horizon. Jacob has returned to his tent, but he cannot sit or be at ease. He walks around the camp, almost panting like a Canaanite dog. His heart is racing.

Jacob realizes his mother never understood his taking possession of the birthright from Esau. He is aware that his brother, by virtue of being the eldest, is entitled to the birthright. It had never occurred to him to question Esau's position in the family. Esau is the elder brother, and frequently protected him from Canaanite and Hittite bullies. When Esau came into the camp from his hunt, empty-handed and hungry, Jacob did not quite believe Esau's urgency for food. As Esau pleaded, more than begging but not quite demanding, in a flash Jacob decided to test out the bargaining he had learned from Itai the Hittite. He observed Esau's body and saw that it was weak and exhausted. He never imagined Esau would yield the birthright, but as Itai had taught him, he asked for more than he thought he could receive. When his brother agreed to give him the birthright for a bowl of red lentils, Jacob knew even then that their father's blessing would seal the birthright for Esau, despite his selling it for a pittance. He suspected that Esau knew that as well.

Jacob never thought his father would recognize and accept the transaction with his brother. Moreover, he could not fathom directly asking Isaac to uphold his deal with Esau. It absolutely never entered his mind to appropriate the blessing with guile and deception.

Jacob's stomach flutters with waves of nausea. His guts are rumbling with anxiety and anticipation of an impending disaster. He is trapped between his father's devotion to Esau's position and his mother's intense determination that he, Jacob, should lead the clan. Isaac's stand, as far as Jacob is concerned, is about the past and the present. Isaac does not wish to repeat Abraham's cruelties, even if they were meant for a good cause. Isaac undoubtedly believes that if he blesses Esau now, he can mentor him as a leader and overcome the influence of the Canaanite wives. Mother has never been open to a deep rapport with Esau. Her worry is only to safeguard the family as a unique clan among the tribes of Canaan. She is wholeheartedly loyal to Gevurah and to the Covenant. Many times, Rebekah has told Esau that Gevurah led her from Haran to Canaan to secure the offspring of Abraham and Isaac as a blessing.

A few deep breaths while his eyes are closed settle Jacob in small measure. He is well aware that Esau neither desires nor is capable of leading their clan. Jacob cannot understand why Isaac does not absorb Esau's disinterest. Jacob decides to follow his mother's charge to him regardless of what may result.

Jacob returns to Rebekah's tent. He tells her he is ready to follow her instructions. She reminds him that what he is about to do is a sacred task. It will be justified throughout the clan's future. Rebekah drapes strips of goat skins on Jacob's arms and around his neck. She puts the clay pot of stew in a blanket together with fresh bread, and places them in Jacob's outstretched arm.

"Go to Isaac, my son. May the power of Gevurah strengthen you. May you appear to your blind father as the one who deserves blessing."

As Jacob makes his way to Isaac's tent laden with stew and bread, he is burdened with a question: "If Gevurah is the source and foundation of truth, how can I commit to Gevurah based on the lie I am about to enact?

"Does my name, Jacob, a heal-grabber and supplanter, point to an entire lifetime of dissimulating and prevaricating? The world is full of liars and deceivers. I pray Gevurah will provide me with a ladder of self-knowledge, with rungs of integrity and congruent deeds. In Your sustaining support, Gevurah, I place my hope."

XXII

Deceit for Destiny

Isaac is meditating in his tent in the late afternoon. Despite his advancing age, or perhaps because of it, Isaac conjures in his mind the presence of Eliezer, his long-deceased mentor. How often over the years has Isaac yearned for his insight and advice. Merely speaking in his mind to long-gone Eliezer yields a harvest of wisdom and direction. No doubt this is what remains of his deep and close bond with Eliezer. It has never vanished.

"Eliezer, I am growing ever more weary of pretending blindness. During the last two years, I have complained of dimming vision. I have leaned on Rebekah and others to guide me. Finally, I claim to be enshrouded in a cocoon of darkness. All of this has been to create a circumstance that makes it possible for Rebekah to displace Esau. I do not think she ever doubted the reality of my feigned blindness. However, her own acute evaluation of what goes on in our family would awaken a thought in her to push Jacob to the birthright. She and I, though we never spoke to each other of such a plan, can blame my blindness for my supposed error in blessing Jacob. It will still pain Esau, but he will not think I intentionally rejected him."

Isaac senses Eliezer affirming the purpose he has conceived and molded for so long. There is no other acceptable way. Eliezer counsels him not to make the deception too easy or comfortable for Jacob.

Jacob enters Isaac's tent and interrupts his meditation.

Jacob says, "My father," in a whisper.

"Who are you, my son?"

Jacob freezes. He thinks, "Indeed, who am I? A deceiver of my father, a sneak, and a liar." Sweat beads on his forehead.

He feels like he is in a furnace under the goat skins.

He is trembling despite engulfing waves of heat. He knows he must answer his father.

"It is me. Esau, your firstborn, has done what you asked. So come and eat the stew so you may bless me wholeheartedly."

"My son, how did you manage to return so quickly from the hunt and to make this stew already?" Jacob feels Isaac's suspicion in his question.

"Gevurah, our God, gave me good fortune and success for your sake, Father!"

"My son, I have rarely heard you refer to Gevurah. I hope this means you have committed to Gevurah over the false god Ba'al. I have awaited your faithfulness to Gevurah. So, now come closer, my son. Let me feel you. Are you indeed my son Esau, or a pretender?"

This is the moment Jacob dreads above all: being touched by his father and possibly recognized for who he is. Isaac intuits Jacob's fear and plays on it as Jacob draws near. Isaac feels his arms and neck, which are covered with goat skins that Esau wears. Isaac takes his time, as though considering the tactile evidence.

Musing aloud with his eyes gazing into a vague distance, Isaac says, "The voice is Jacob's voice, but the hands are like Esau's, hairy. May you be blessed, Esau."

Jacob is astonished. Though his arms and hands are covered with goat skins to simulate Esau's mantle of hair, Jacob is smaller and of delicate bones. How could his father not tell? Yet Isaac recognizes his voice. "Is Father not persuaded of my Esau identity? Is he about to unmask me and curse me?"

"Is it really you, my son, Esau?"

"It is I."

"Then bring me your stew, that I may eat and then give you my heartfelt blessing."

Jacob places a bowl of stew before Isaac. His father savors it, eating leisurely, and asks for more. "Thank you, my son, for this Yevus gazelle stew. It is a delicacy. Now pour me some wine."

Jacob thinks it is strange that his father appreciates the goat stew as though it were of gazelle. The flavors are so different. Gazelle is Isaac's long suit. Blind people usually have more acuity of their other senses. "How can Isaac not tell he is eating goat meat? Has Father lost his taste and smell along with his vision? He recognized my voice but not my footsteps when I entered his tent. My gait is so very different than Esau's."

Jacob arises from the mat to clear the bowl and utensils. As he moves to wrap what he brought, he feels as though Isaac is watching him, following his movements in the tent.

"Come here and kiss me, my son."

Jacob comes over and kisses him. As he does so, Jacob glances into his father's eyes. They look clear and focused.

Isaac inhales the scent of Jacob's garments, which belong to Esau, and tells him to sit. Isaac now bestows the birthright blessing upon him.

"Look, the scent of my son is like the scent of a field blessed by Gevurah. May Gevurah grant you the dew of heaven, the riches of the earth, an abundance of grain, and new wine. Let people serve you and nations bow to you. Be master over your kin and let your relatives bow down to you. Curse those who curse you, and may those who bless you be blessed."

Jacob leaves Isaac's tent and brings the bowls back to Rebekah's tent.

"My son, did it go well for you? Did Isaac give you his blessing?"

"Mother, deceiving Father turned my soul inside out. I was nearly certain he knew I am Jacob. He ate the stew, and I have received the blessing and the birthright."

"Praise Gevurah, who has guided our steps!"

"Father deserves praise as well."

"How do you mean that, Jacob?"

"Mother, I am not of the opinion that Father is blind. His failing then vanishing eyesight has been the greatest deception beyond anything you have planned or I have carried out.

"I believe he was emotionally blind when he clung to the hope Esau would become our clan leader. When the blindness of his bias cleared, he adopted physical blindness as an excuse to release himself without guilt from blessing Esau."

Just then, they hear a loud wailing and then a piercing cry coming from Isaac's tent. Esau is with Isaac. He presents him with the gazelle stew he has hunted. He now seeks his father's blessing.

Esau's animal-like cries come when Isaac tells him he has already bestowed the birthright blessing on one whom he thought was his firstborn son. Esau knows who came to Isaac's tent. He does not doubt that it was Jacob who, through guile and deception, robbed him of the birthright blessing.

Esau grits his teeth. He clamps his jaws shut, and his cheeks bulge. Through his barely parted lips, he says, "Father, don't you have one more blessing for me? Bless me also, Father!"

"Your brother came with guile. He stole the birthright and your blessing. I have blessed him. I made him master over you. I cannot retract my blessing of what Gevurah will bestow upon him."

"Oh, Father, surely you can give me a blessing as well."

Esau's pain bubbles inside him. He is a boiling cauldron. He envisions his hands around Jacob's neck, his thumbs crushing Jacob's lying throat. His father's presence in front of him leads him to do no harm to Jacob while Isaac yet lives. After his father's passing, there will be means for revenge on the great clan leader, Jacob.

Isaac pulls Esau to himself. Esau is drooling, and his nose gushes with snot. His chest heaves, and he takes gulps of air. Isaac has words. He is there for his elder son. He hopes to calm and comfort him. When Isaac feels Esau breathe evenly and his body relaxing, he speaks to Esau.

"My son, I have a blessing for you. I hope it will provide a shield for you and your descendants. I can only speak it in the name of Gevurah. I hope you will accept Gevurah and the divine blessing I convey. If so, bow your head before me."

Isaac places his hands on Esau's head. He blesses:

> "Your dwelling will occupy the rich places of the earth
> with the dew of heaven upon it.
> You will serve your brother,
> yet when you become restless
> you will break his yoke from your neck."

When Rebekah hears Esau's shouts and cries, she leads Jacob away to a place beyond the goat pens. They are in a remote, private space. Anyone in the vicinity could not hear Rebekah's words over the raucous bleating of scores of goats.

"Son, listen to me well. You must leave our tents and this camp tomorrow. I do not know what vengeance Esau is plotting, but he will not soon let this matter go. You must go to your uncle Laban, my brother in Paddan Aram. He will welcome you, but beware of his wiles. He uses and exploits people, even family members. You must marry within our clan. Those women do not worship Gevurah, but you can teach them. When you bring them back here, they will have no one but you to rely upon. They will have no alternative but to accept Gevurah and our Covenant. I will pack provisions for your journey. It will be long and arduous, but you are strong and able. Go bid farewell to Isaac at tomorrow's first light."

"Mother, I will do as you bid me. I do fear Esau's rage, which is not uncalled for. But if I leave Canaan, how do I avail myself and our family of Gevurah's promise to give this land to me and my offspring?"

"Jacob, you must trust in Gevurah. Even if your days in Paddan Aram are many and lengthen into years, Gevurah will bring you home. You leave here empty—without a wife or children, without possessions, without worldly experience, and with insufficient confidence in Gevurah. My heart tells me Gevurah will eventually bring you back to Canaan full, with wives, numerous children, great wealth, and supreme trust in your partnership with Gevurah. Esau will no longer hold his grudge, for he will have his own blessings. You will dwell securely in the shade of Gevurah's protection."

As dawn lightens, the sky promises hope to Rebekah. She goes to Isaac. She pretends she knows nothing of Jacob's deceit or of Esau's distraught fury.

"My husband, I cannot divert my mind from worrying day and night that Jacob, like Esau, will take a Canaanite or a Hittite woman to marry. Just as Abraham sent Eliezer to Haran to find a wife for you, please send Jacob to Paddan Aram to our family. I am sure Gevurah will guide him to a wife who is fertile and fitting."

"As you advise, Rebekah, so will I do. Send Jacob to me that I may bless him before he departs."

. . .

Jacob obeys his father's summons. A goat skin bag of provisions Rebekah has packed is on his shoulder. Isaac repeats Rebekah's idea that Jacob should go to Paddan Aram to avoid marrying out of the clan. He does not mention the deceit or the murderous anger of Esau.

"Bow your head, my son, that I may give you my real and true blessing, the one that is made for you.

"May Gevurah bless you, make you fertile and multiply you.

"May you become an assembly of peoples.

"May Gevurah give you the blessing of Abraham in all things, to you, to your offspring, to possess the land of your dwelling."

Jacob and Isaac hug and kiss, then Jacob hurries from the tent to his destiny in Paddan Aram.

We will leave the detailed stories of Jacob and Esau for another occasion. Esau will relocate to Seir, the red rock country east of the Jordan and overlooking the Sea of Salt. He will become a mighty warrior and an honest ruler. Jacob will reach Paddan Aram, marry his cousins Leah and Rachel, and work for his uncle Laban for twenty years until his return to Canaan. He is summoned back home, not by El Shaddai, nor by Gevurah, but by his God, El Elohei Yisrael. His God is the source of bold action and risk to attain a future of purpose and fulfillment.

XXIII

Wholeness Unbound

Isaac does not recall a time in his life when he has felt the conflicted emotions that swirl in him after blessing Jacob and Esau. The wailing, pleading cry of Esau, "Father, have you not reserved a blessing for me?" reverberates in his mind. After providing for a lifetime an extra measure of love to his elder son, who lacked a depth of mother's love, Isaac pulled the emotional foundation from under Esau. Jacob clearly has shown the family feeling and responsibility to lead Gevurah's people. He is smart, sensitive, and clever. That is his strength. It makes him worthy to bear the Covenant. That is his weakness as well. He steps on people to achieve his aims and uses stratagems to realize his goals.

Isaac's heart pains him. It is, at times, like a sack of clay shards whose sharp edges inflict twinges of guilt. When he reflects on pretending blindness, he is cold and numb as a frigid desert night wind. Isaac knows from the center of his being that he had no choice but to transmit the Covenantal blessing to Jacob. By so doing, Isaac was aligning his affirmation of Gevurah and his values of truth and righteousness with his actions and his life's purpose. Isaac is well aware of the necessity of reframing and making congruent his values and deeds, his obligations and actions. Such an awareness does not reduce the agony of the steps he has taken.

Even knowing the nature of the struggle he has experienced and understanding the maze of conflicting feelings, he is not entirely comforted and calm. For Isaac, healing only comes through meditation outside his tent in nature's habitat.

Isaac leaves his tent. He claims to his family and to the servants that Gevurah has restored his sight. He refers to it as a divine gift. He walks beyond his goat pens and fields to the uncultivated desert land. He inhales the pungent and spicy scents of acacia and creosote, of prickly pear cactus, grasses, and the green odor of stubborn cyclamen peeking between the rocks. It is as though the perfumes of the desert shrubs and bushes are sharing their spirits and vitality with him. He begins to feel renewed and restored. He resolves to continue his desert walks each day. Clearly, the spirit of growing plants around him expands his own spirit and refreshes him. He feels they reach out to embrace him and seek his welfare. Isaac offers a prayer of gratitude for creation and for the natural world in which he shares.

Isaac comes to a boulder low enough to sit on with a depression in its surface, which makes it a comfortable seat. Behind it is a larger rock that partially shields Isaac's stone seat from the sun's intense rays. He sits. He closes his eyes. He opens his ears to the calls and conversations of the myriad bird species, domestic and migrating. As though on the wings of eagles, Isaac is uplifted to a plane of inner space. He envisions around himself the presence of precious beings near to him yet at physical distance. He is part of a circle. He looks around. Eliezer is there, gazing at Isaac, a slight smile on the old servant's countenance. Melchizedek, his guide and teacher, king of Yevus, nods encouragement in Isaac's direction. Ishmael and Rebekah sit in the circle with looks of anticipation. None of them speaks aloud, but Isaac hears their messages within his mind.

"Isaac," says Melchizedek, "you are unbound! You are unbound from the Moriah altar. You are unbound from your resentment of Abraham. You are unbound from El Shaddai."

Ishmael focuses on his younger half-brother's mind.

"Isaac, you are unbound from guilt, from my exile, though you brought none of it about. Your reconciling outreach binds us as brothers, and they are chosen bonds of love. You are unbound from the past."

Eliezer addresses Isaac.

"You are unbound from a divided spirit. You released Esau and transmitted to Jacob the Covenant that you affirm. You are unbound from false promises and the danger of hypocrisy."

"My husband," says Rebekah, "You are whole and unbound except for our bond to each other and to Gevurah."

Isaac thinks, "I am bound to each of you in love. You are my blessings, my encouragement, my boundless support."

Isaac continues to sit overwhelmed with gratitude for the gifts of those who have surrounded him all his life. They have helped him mend what was shattered in his life, repair relationships, and make himself whole.

Isaac gets up from his rock to head back to his tent. He is calm and full. Then he beholds a sight that adds to his joy. Rebekah is standing at the entrance of his tent. Her water jug, the one she brought so long ago from Paddan Aram, made by Aunt Milcah, is by her side. She dips a trimmed cedar branch into the jar. She withdraws the branch. She sprinkles the blessed water of the jug all around Isaac's tent—over it, at its entrance, and on the ground on which it is set. Can there be a greater expression of blessing?

As Isaac walks toward Rebekah and the tent, forked lightning illumines the camp and thunder pierces the quiet evening. Rare drops of rain fall. The number of drops and pace of the rain quicken into a Negev deluge. The parched land that was cracked like an earthen mosaic is now smooth and whole. Contented, Isaac laughs.

About the Author

PAUL J. CITRIN RECEIVED a bachelor's degree in history from UCLA in 1968. He did a year of independent study in Israel in 1972. He was ordained as a rabbi by the Hebrew Union College in 1973. He has primarily served as a spiritual leader in congregations. His focus has been on education, social justice, and Israel. He has written books on children's liturgy, theology, and fiction. He and his wife, Susan Morrison Citrin, are retired in Albuquerque, New Mexico.

Printed in the USA
CPSIA information can be obtained
at www.ICGtesting.com
LVHW082043060823
754441LV00005B/198

9 781666 777482